Broken Mirror

And Other Stories

An Anthology by

Jacqueline E. Smith

Wind Trail Publishing

Broken Mirror and Other Stories

Wind Trail Publishing
PO Box 830851
Richardson, TX 75083-0851
www.WindTrailPublishing.com

First Paperback Edition, August 2019

ISBN-13: 978-1-0874787-2-2
ISBN-10: 1-0874-7872-3

Cover Design: Wind Trail Publishing

This is a work of fiction. Characters, places, and incidents portrayed in
this novel are either products of the author's imagination or used
fictitiously.

In loving memory of my beautiful Midnight.
My miracle kitty, my writing companion, my best friend.
I love you forever, Baby Girl. I'll see you at the Rainbow
Bridge.

Table of Contents

Broken Mirror

Broken Mirror
In the woods,
Show me what you see.
A face I know
I've never known
Staring back at me.

"Okay, Wild Geese! It's time for a water break!" Christine announced.

It was a beautiful summer's day at Camp Shady Spruce and the campers of Cabin 3B, the Wild Geese, were on their way to archery.

"Water break!" Christine's co-counselor, Harper echoed.

One by one, their eight campers pulled out their water bottles and began to drink. Christine and Harper did the same. Even beneath the shade of a thousand trees and their saplings, the Texoma heat was sweltering. Staying hydrated was essential.

"Great job, Wild Geese! Now, I want to see everyone take one more big gulp and then we're off to archery! Who's excited?" Harper asked.

All seven girls cheered.

Wait, seven? Christine thought. *That can't be right.*

She counted again, but again, she counted seven.

"Harper, hold up," Christine said. "We're missing someone."

"What?" Harper asked, scanning the faces of their campers.

It was only their second day of camp and although Christine made a point to memorize names and faces early on, it still took more than a glance to figure out who was absent.

"Miss Chrissy?" One of the little girls raised her hand. "Abigail isn't here."

Abigail. As soon as Christine heard the name, she could see the child's face as clear as day; wide, angelic eyes, a button nose, and a soft scattering of freckles. She was a sweet girl, but very quiet. A girl who could have very well slipped away unnoticed.

"Oh, God," Harper gasped.

"It's okay. Don't panic. I'm sure she's fine," Christine said, trying to reassure herself as much as Harper and the girls. "Did anyone see where she went?"

"She said she saw something," another one of their campers, Mikayla, spoke up.

"Where?" Christine asked.

"In the woods."

That was no help. They were surrounded by woods. But the trail from their cabin to archery was relatively short. Christine could easily retrace their steps. Hopefully, Abigail hadn't strayed too far.

"Okay, I'm going to go back and look for her," she said. "Harper, go ahead and take the girls to archery, but let Sandy and Kip know what's happened. I'll call you on the radio when I find her."

And with that, Christine took off running back up the trail, calling out Abigail's name and keeping a desperate eye out for anything that looked out of place. She wracked her brain for her last memory of the girl. She knew Abigail had been there when they'd left their cabin, and when they'd stopped to watch a red-headed woodpecker tap away on a tree trunk in search of bugs. In fact, Christine remembered the exact tree. It was the large oak with the trail markers, and it was close. That meant Abigail couldn't have gotten far.

Sure enough, just a few paces past the oak tree, Christine noticed a scattering of leaves that had been disrupted. It could have been an animal, or even the wind, but Christine needed to believe that it wasn't. This had to be Abigail's path.

I'm going to find her. She's fine. Everything is going to be fine.

A few meters off the trail, Christine caught a glimpse of a bright purple baseball cap through the trees and saplings.

"Abigail?" Christine called.

The little girl didn't respond. As Christine approached her, she could see that Abigail was standing motionless with her back to the trail. It was almost like she was in some sort of trance.

Careful not to alarm her, Christine spoke her name again.

"Abigail?"

It was only then that Christine saw the mirror.

Strange. She'd hiked these woods at least a dozen times. She'd never seen the mirror, or anything like it.

It was clearly an antique and, from the look of it, had endured long exposure to the elements. The mirror itself was cracked and caked with filth and grime. Its intricate bronze frame was tarnished and covered in dirt and cobwebs. But Abigail didn't even seem to notice the mirror's state of disrepair. She simply stood stock-still, silent as the summer air, her eyes locked on her own reflection.

"Hey." Christine reached out and gently touched Abigail's shoulder.

The little girl jumped and turned wide, frightened eyes on her counselor.

"Are you okay?" Christine asked. "We've been looking all over for you."

"Sorry," Abigail whispered.

3

"It's okay," Christine assured her. "But you've got to stay with the group, okay? It's not safe out here if you're all by yourself."

"I know."

"Good. Now, what do you say we head over to archery?"

Abigail merely nodded. Then, she took one last look in the mirror.

Christine, meanwhile, grabbed her radio and called Sandy and Kip over at archery.

"*Go for Kip.*"

"Kip, hey, it's Christine. I found Abigail. She's safe and sound. We're on our way."

"*10-4. Glad to hear it.*"

Finally, Christine took Abigail's hand.

"Come on, Sweetie," she said.

And together, they made their way back to the trail, out of the woods, and away from the mysterious broken mirror.

Evenings at Camp Shady Spruce were peaceful. The golden glow of the setting sun cast shadows dancing through the trees while insects serenaded the night's return. And with each passing minute, a new star twinkled to life in the vast, open sky.

Once the lights went out in the girls' room, Harper went straight to bed herself. Christine, however, grabbed a book and a flashlight and slipped outside to their cabin's front porch. Savoring the silence and the brief moment of glorious solitude, Christine took a deep breath and sat down in one of the old, rickety rocking chairs. There, she opened her book and read until she heard footsteps traveling down the graveled path toward Cabin 3B.

"All the Wild Geese asleep?" Kip asked, taking a seat next to Christine.

"Yep. They were exhausted. Especially since a lot of them didn't sleep well last night." First nights for the younger kids were always the hardest.

"I hope they had fun today."

"They did. Especially at archery," Christine winked.

"We try," Kip grinned. Then, he leaned in and kissed her lightly on the lips.

Christine blushed. They weren't together. Not really. They'd become friends last summer and had flirted a bit, but at the end of the summer, they'd gone their separate ways. And even though Christine was all but certain that once this summer ended, they'd say goodbye again, she was happy to enjoy his company, and his kisses, while she could.

"So, how's Abigail doing?" Kip asked.

"She seems okay. A little quiet, maybe, but she was shy even before she got lost."

"Do you know why she wandered off? Is she homesick?"

"No. At least, I don't think so," Christine said. "She uh... she actually saw something."

"What was it?"

Christine hadn't told anyone about the mirror, in part because she honestly couldn't figure out how. An antique mirror just standing in the middle of the woods? It sounded crazy, even to her ears. But maybe Kip would have some insight as to how it had come to be there.

"A mirror."

"A mirror?" Kip asked, looking confused. "What do you mean, a mirror? Like, a little handheld mirror?"

"No. Like a full length, standup, broken mirror."

"But that... that's so weird. How did it get there?"

"I was hoping you might know."

"I have no idea."

Just then, a shrill scream pierced the night. Stricken with fear and panic, Christine leapt up out of her chair and bolted back inside the cabin where Harper was already tending to the girls.

"What's going on?" Christine asked.

At a glance, nothing seemed out of place. Well, except for the campers who were sitting up in their bunk beds and rubbing their poor, tired eyes. Then she noticed one little girl, in particular, had buried her face in her hands. Her small body was wracked with sobs.

Abigail.

"Hey, Sweetie," Harper whispered, kneeling down next to her. "Are you okay?"

Abigail shook her head.

"What's wrong? Did you have a nightmare?"

"Someone's... out there..." Abigail whispered through her tears.

"What?" Christine asked.

"Out where?" Harper pressed.

Slowly, Abigail lifted a trembling hand and pointed toward the window closest to her bed.

"I heard them... scratching," she whimpered.

"Did anyone else hear it?" Christine asked her campers. They shook their heads.

"Maybe it was a tree branch," Harper said. "It does get a little windy out here at night."

That, Christine thought, *or someone really was out there.*

For two weeks now, the counselor of Camp Shady Spruce had been engaged in an unofficial prank war. Last week, for example, Christine, Harper, and the other girls had ambushed the guys with water balloons while the campers played Capture the Flag. Even though cabins were supposed to be off-limits, Christine wouldn't have been surprised if a few of the guys, Alec and Gunther in particular, decided to overstep their boundaries.

She made a mental note to interrogate them in the morning. Her campers needed her tonight.

Forgotten Mirror
In the woods
Who left you here to stand
Alone when shadows
Come to life
And darkness is at hand?

The next morning, Christine cornered Alec and Gunther in the dining hall.

"Hey, can I talk to you guys for a sec?" she asked.

"Make it quick. We're supposed to be down at the waterfront in eight minutes," Gunther told her. Christine resisted the urge to roll her eyes. Gunther didn't care about punctuality. He cared about Victoria, the gorgeous new lifeguard. For that reason alone, Christine was tempted to make him wait. Recalling the terrified look on Abigail's face, however, she quickly decided against it.

"Were either of you outside our cabin last night?" she asked.

"No. Though we couldn't help but notice a certain archery instructor sauntering down after lights-out," Alec remarked.

"Okay, I don't want to talk about Kip. I just want to know if either one of you were outside scratching on the windows."

"Why would we do that?" Gunther asked.

"I don't know. You thought it might be fun to scare us?"

"Well, yeah, it's always fun to scare you. But we're not going to slink around your cabin the middle of the night. That's just creepy," Gunter said.

"Out of curiosity, why do you ask?" Alec asked.

"One of the girls thought she heard something last night."

"Are you sure it wasn't you and Kip making - "

"She heard someone scratching on her window," Christine snapped, cutting Gunther off before he could make any inappropriate though not entirely inaccurate accusations.

"Scratching?" Alec asked.

"It was probably a tree branch," Gunther said.

"That's what Harper said," Christine admitted.

"So why are you interrogating us?" Gunther pressed.

"I just wanted to make sure."

"Yeah, right. You were hoping it was us so you'd have an excuse to yell at us," Gunther said. "I know you, Christine. I know you have it out for us."

"You got me, Gunther," Christine shrugged.

Then, she turned away and made her way back to Harper and the Wild Geese. She knew she should feel relieved that Alec and Gunther hadn't been lurking outside their cabin window, and a part of her did. But the other part had secretly hoped it had been them, because then at least she'd have an explanation.

You have an explanation, she reminded herself. *It was a tree branch.*

But try as she might, she couldn't shake the feeling that it was something else entirely. Something to do with a secret in the shadows, a reflection in the forest, and the shattered glass of a forgotten mirror.

For the rest of the day, Christine kept a close eye on Abigail. Every once in a while, the little girl would glance over her shoulder, but for the most part, she seemed to be enjoying herself. She participated in all the low ropes team-building games. She made a bracelet for her big sister in arts and crafts. She even went back for a second s'more at campfire that evening. By the time night fell, Christine finally felt herself beginning to relax.

"Okay, girls! Lights-out is in five minutes! Make sure your PJs are on and your teeth are brushed!" Harper announced.

A few of the girls climbed into bed and snuggled beneath their blankets immediately, while others huddled in the corners of their room, whispering and giggling. Then there was Abigail, who sat crisscrossed on her bed, clutching her stuffed bunny and staring out the window.

Christine knelt down next to her.

"Hey, sweetie," she said. "Did you have fun today?"

Abigail nodded.

"What was your favorite part?"

"I liked the s'mores," Abigail answered without looking her in the eye.

"Me, too. I *love* s'mores," Christine smiled. Abigail didn't respond. "Hey, listen, I know last night was a little scary. But you know that Harper and I would never let anything happen to you, right?"

Again, Abigail nodded.

"Good. Now, if you hear anything or if you see anything or if you get scared in the middle of the night, don't be afraid to come get me or Harper okay? That's what we're here for; to protect you and to make you feel safe."

Abigail sniffled and hugged her bunny closer. Christine knew she was done talking, but she hoped that the little girl would at least take her words to heart.

Once the lights went out, Christine slipped back outside. Instead of settling in with a book and waiting for Kip, however, she took her flashlight and walked the perimeter of their cabin. She didn't exactly know what she was looking for, but she was determined to find it. If it was out there.

Alas, there was nothing. No footprints. No broken branches. Just the hum of insects and the tranquil stillness of night.

Heaving a sigh of resignation, Christine made her way back to the front porch to find Kip sitting in his usual rocking chair.

"Hey," he smiled as she approached. "There you are. Everything okay?"

"Yeah..." she replied, taking the seat next to him.

"You don't sound so sure about that."

"I'm just worried about Abigail."

"How did she do today?" Kip asked.

"She actually did pretty okay. But tonight, she seemed a little... distant."

"She's probably tired."

"I hope that's it. It would be great if she could get a good night's sleep."

"That probably goes for you, too," Kip observed.

"Maybe," Christine sighed.

If it had been any other night, any other week, any other summer, she wouldn't have even been considering going to bed so early, especially with Kip there. She would have been suggesting midnight hikes down to the secret cove behind their cabin or a romantic evening of stargazing from the deck of the high-ropes course. Anything for just a few more moments alone with Kip.

Except... they weren't alone. Someone else was out there. Christine could hear them shuffling through the brush and fallen leaves.

"Listen," she whispered to Kip. "Do you hear that?"

"What?" Kip asked.

But Christine didn't answer. Instead, she stood up, stepped off the porch, and looked around for any signs of movement. At first, she couldn't see anything out of the ordinary through the pitch darkness. Just the shadowy silhouettes of the forest against the gentle glow of the night sky.

But then, there *was* something. Something small, running through the trees on quick feet.

A child.

No. That was impossible. All the kids were in bed. Or at least, they were supposed to be.

"Hello?" Christine called out.

"What's going on?" Kip asked, sprinting to her side.

"I think there's a camper out of bed."

"Do you want me to request a headcount? I have my radio."

"Yeah, go for it," Christine told him absently. She'd lost sight of the figure in the woods and her heart and mind were racing. Hastily, she reached for her flashlight and shone its beam into the heart of the forest.

Nothing. There was nothing.

Then, another ear-splitting wail arose from inside Cabin 3B.

"Oh, not again," Christine pleaded before racing back inside.

The scene was a familiar one. The lights were on, the girls were awake, and Harper was kneeling next to poor, sweet Abigail. The only difference was tonight, Abigail was inconsolable.

"Hey, hey, it's okay," Harper was telling her. "Calm down."

"I... I..." the little girl was sobbing so hard she could barely speak.

"You're okay. You're safe. Just take deep breaths for me, okay? Deep breaths," Harper instructed.

"Should we call the nurse?" Christine asked.

"Don't..." Abigail choked out.

"Don't what, sweetheart?" Harper asked.

"Don't... let... her get me," Abigail wept.

"Who?" Christine asked.

"Me!" Abigail cried out.

Harper turned around and exchanged a rather hopeless glance with Christine.

Once Abigail and the rest of the girls had finally settled back down, Christine and Harper retreated to their bedroom.

"What are we going to do?" Christine asked, keeping her voice low so the girls wouldn't hear her.

"I don't know," Harper sighed.

"Should we call her parents?"

"Maybe. If nothing else, we at least need to report what's been going on to Tracy and Julie." Tracy and Julie were the program leaders and the counselors' bosses.

"Agree," Christine said.

Tap, tap, tap.

A soft rapping on their window startled them both.

"What the - " Harper breathed.

"It's Kip." Christine suddenly remembered she had left her beau outside for the second night in a row.

Quietly, she slipped back outside.

"Hey," he whispered. "Is everything okay?"

"Yeah, just... Abigail's having another rough night."

"Well, listen, I radioed all the cabins. All campers are present and accounted for."

"You mean..."

"There was no one out here tonight."

"But I - I heard them. I saw them," Christine insisted.

"I believe you," Kip assured her. "But maybe it wasn't what you thought. Maybe it was a deer. Or a tall bobcat."

"A tall bobcat? Really?"

"Well, whatever it was, it wasn't a camper. I don't know if that puts your mind at ease at all..."

It didn't, but Christine had neither the energy nor the heart to tell him. Instead, she wrapped her arms around his shoulders, buried her face in his neck, and breathed him in, as though he and he alone could alleviate every doubt, every uncertainty, every fear.

"All right, Wild Geese, rise and shine! Up and at 'em!" Christine sang.

After a long, restless night, she doubted any of her campers were all that eager to start the new day, but she and Harper agreed they had to try to keep things as normal and upbeat as possible.

Even though the girls were noticeably sleepy, they climbed out of bed and got themselves dressed without complaint. Thirty minutes later, they were on their way to the dining hall for breakfast.

While the girls took their seats at their assigned table, Christine made a beeline for the instant coffee maker. She usually tried not to indulge too much when camp was in session, but she knew she needed a pick-me-up if she was going to make it through the day. Even after just a few sips, she was beginning to feel more alert, more herself.

It was only then that she took her first real look at her campers that morning. Back at the cabin, she'd been so preoccupied with getting them up and out the door that she hadn't taken the time to really notice them. Now, under the florescent light of the dining hall, she was relieved to see they all looked far more cheerful and awake than she'd originally perceived.

All, that is, except for Abigail. She sat at the far end of the table, keeping quietly to herself and staring down at her lap. A lock of her hair fell into her tired eyes, casting a dark shadow across her face.

Except -

No. It wasn't a shadow.

Christine barely registered the coffee mug slipping out of her hand as she bolted across the dining hall to Abigail.

"Christine, what is it?" Harper asked urgently.

"Abigail?" Christine said, dropping to her knees in front of her camper. "Abigail, sweetie, I need you to look at me."

Slowly, Abigail lifted her head up to meet Christine's eye. As she did, Christine gasped in horror.

Ugly, purple bruises were blossoming all over the little girl's face and neck.

"Oh, my God," Harper whispered. "Abigail, what happened?"

"I did it," Abigail whimpered.

"What do you mean?" Christine asked. "Did you fall? Hurt yourself?"

"No. It was *me*," Abigail insisted, fighting back tears.

"I don't understand. Why would you do that?" Harper asked.

"I don't know," Abigail wailed and buried her face in Christine's shirt.

Feeling helpless, Christine looked to Harper for answers, but her friend looked just as lost.

After breakfast, Christine and Harper dropped their Wild Geese off for their session in the music room before requesting an emergency meeting with Tracy and Julie. They agreed to meet in the counselor's lounge. There, their bosses sat and listened while Christine and Harper recounted the events of the last few days, everything from Abigail wandering off on the way to archery to her night terrors to the troubling bruises on her face.

"We need to talk with her," Julie said. "We'll stop by Cabin 3B after lunch during Turtle Time. Abigail may not be inclined to tell us who's hurting her, but one of the other girls just might be willing."

Christine, Harper, and Tracy all nodded in agreement.

It wasn't until the meeting had been adjourned and she and Harper were heading back to pick the girls up from music that Christine realized something. Throughout their entire conversation about Abigail, neither she nor Harper had made any mention of the mirror.

Magic Mirror
In the woods
The time has come to tell

14

Secrets, whispers
That you've kept
And hidden here so well.

Turtle Time was the time of day that campers bemoaned and counselors relished. It was the hour after lunch when everyone retreated to their cabins for a few glorious moments of rest while the sun was at its highest and the summer air at its hottest.

Usually, Christine would take a quick nap or sit and read while the girls lounged in their bunks, listening to music or writing in their journals. Today, however, they all sat in a circle on the floor of the girls' room, listening to Julie and Tracy as they talked about bullying and boundaries.

"All we want is for everyone here at Camp Shady Spruce to feel welcome and safe. Now, we've been told that a few of our campers have been having a hard time sleeping, and that some of you are even getting hurt in the middle of the night," Tracy said. "If there's anything that anyone wants to tell us, we promise you we won't get mad. You won't be in trouble. We just need to know."

The girls all looked around at one another. Christine held her breath while she waited for someone to speak up.

Finally, a little girl named Sofia raised her hand.

"Someone's hurting Abigail," she said.

"Is this true?" Julie asked.

"Yes," Mikayla spoke up. "She's scaring her."

"Who is it?" Tracy asked.

The room fell silent.

"Girls, we know you're here to have fun. And whoever's doing this, I'm sure you just think you're playing a joke. But scaring someone... leaving bruises... it's very harmful. And it needs to stop."

Again, the girls exchanged glances, but this time, it was Abigail who broke the silence.

"Nthm," she mumbled down to the floor.

15

"What was that, Abigail?" Julie asked.

"It's not *them*," Abigail repeated. "It's me."

"That's what she was saying earlier," Christine muttered to Tracy.

"Abigail, honey, what do you mean it's you?"

"It's *me*." The little girl began to cry. Then she hung her head and whimpered, "I want to go home."

"Oh, sweetie..." Christine's heart broke for her camper.

"What should we do? Should we call her parents?" Harper asked, keeping her voice low.

"It might be for the best," Julie said.

"I'll head up to the main office and make the call," Tracy told them. "In the meantime, just go about your day, stick to your schedule, give the girls a sense of stability. We don't want the rest of the campers worrying or getting upset."

Christine and Harper agreed, and ten minutes later, the Wild Geese of Cabin 3B had changed into their swimsuits and were on their way down to the lake for Free Swim.

While Harper joined the kids down at the dock, Christine took a seat on the shore. To her utter dismay, it didn't take long for Alec and Gunther to join her.

"So, did'ja ever catch that creeper who was running around your cabin last night?" Gunther asked. "Or was it just Kip?"

"Ha, you're funny," Christine grumbled, hugging her knees to her chest.

Gunther frowned.

"Hey, you know I'm just messin' with you, right?"

"Yeah, I know," Christine sighed.

"So, what's going on?" Alec asked.

"We're just having a lot of problems with one of the girls," Christine explained. "Tracy is actually calling her parents to see if they can come and get her."

"Oh, man. You serious?" Gunther asked.

"What kind of problems?" Alec wanted to know.

For the second time that day, Christine shared Abigail's strange story. As she did, both Alec and Gunther took a closer look at the little girl drawing circles in the sand.

"What happened to her face?" Gunther asked.

"I have no idea. We can't get a straight answer out of her," Christine told them. "She keeps saying, 'It was me. I did it.' You know, like she, herself. But that just doesn't make sense, does it?"

"She probably covering up for another kid," Gunther said, leaning back on his elbows.

"Or she's seen her doppelgänger," Alec remarked.

"Her what?" Christine asked.

"You know, her doppelgänger. Her mirror image."

Christine perked up at the word *mirror*.

"Shut up, Alec. You're such a nerd," Gunther groaned.

"No, no. I'm interested," Christine said. "What do you mean, her mirror image?"

"Christine, it was just a joke," Alec said.

"Humor me, then."

Alec took a deep breath.

"So, according to folklore, a doppelgänger is a spirit, a ghostly entity, that looks exactly like you. It's considered by some to be a harbinger of bad luck, but there are others who believe that if you come face-to-face with your doppelgänger..." That's when Alec trailed off, seemingly uncertain whether or not he should continue.

"What?" Christine pressed.

"It's just a story, Christine."

"Alec. Tell me."

Alec heaved a reluctant sigh.

"There are those who say that if you meet your doppelgänger... then... death is imminent."

In spite of the sweltering Texoma heat, Christine felt her blood run ice cold.

"No," she breathed. "No. That can't be right."

"Christine, chill. It isn't real," Gunther reminded her.

"No, I know that," Christine replied weakly, rubbing her eyes with the heels of her hands.

It wasn't real. It *couldn't* be real. Whatever was happening with Abigail wasn't paranormal. Mystifying, perhaps. But not mythical. It wasn't possible.

It couldn't be.

That evening, Tracy asked to meet Christine and Harper outside their cabin.

"What's going on?" Harper asked. "Are Abigail's parents on their way?"

"I couldn't get a hold of them," Tracy answered. "I left messages on both their cell phones and at her dad's office, but so far, no one's called me back."

"So, what are we going to do?" Christine asked.

"There's nothing we can do. Except wait," Tracy said. "How has she been today?"

"Quiet," Harper responded.

"Any new bruises?" Tracy asked.

"Not that we've seen," Christine said.

"And Christine has been watching her like a hawk," Harper added.

"Well, the minute I hear from them, I'll come and let you know. Until then, just take care of her. Like I know you do," Tracy said.

"We're trying," Harper sighed.

"Yeah, and I'm not sure we're succeeding," Christine said.

"You are," Tracy assured them. "She couldn't be in better hands."

Christine hoped she was right. Sunset was fast-approaching, and she wasn't sure if she or her campers could take another night of restlessness and uncertainty.

As it happened, the Wild Geese were so exhausted after their day of fun in the sun that most of them were showered and tucked away in their bunks before the lights were even out. Abigail must have been particularly wiped out, because by the time Christine and Harper looked in to say goodnight, she was already fast asleep.

Feeling elated and more than a little relieved, Christine fell into bed herself. As much as she would have loved to meet Kip outside, she was so exhausted she could barely keep her eyes open. Within moments, she succumbed to deep, dark, and dreamless slumber.

Christine didn't know what it was that woke her.

She barely even remembered falling asleep in the first place.

All she was aware of, as she struggled to make sense of the dizzying darkness, was the cold. The strange, unnatural chill that left her shivering in her bed.

"Christine?" Harper whispered. "What's going on? It's freezing."

"I don't know," Christine replied. "Maybe it's the air conditioner."

"I'll check the thermostat," Harper murmured, switching on her flashlight and climbing out of bed.

"While you do that, I'm going to go look in on the girls," Christine said.

Ordinarily, she wouldn't have wanted to risk disturbing them, but the shock of waking up to an icy wind sweeping through the cabin had left her feeling unnerved. She needed to make sure her girls were okay, or at least that they had enough blankets.

As she had suspected, they were all awake, sitting up in bed and whispering to each other.

"Miss Chrissy," one of them called out when they saw her. "Why is it so cold?"

"I don't know," she replied gently. "Harper's trying to turn down the air conditioning."

And she must have succeeded. Already, the biting chill was beginning to subside.

Moments later, Harper appeared.

"How's it feeling in here?" she whispered.

"Better," Christine answered. "What was going on with the thermostat?"

"That's the weird part," Harper replied. "There doesn't seem to be anything wrong with it. It was set to 72, same as always."

"But that doesn't make sense," Christine murmured.

"We can have maintenance come by and take a look at it tomorrow, just to be sure. But for now, I think we should be okay."

Christine nodded and turned back to their campers.

"Is everyone feeling better?" she asked them.

Several small voices responded with, "Yes."

"Good. Well then, we're going to go back to our room, but remember if you need anything, don't hesitate to - "

"Abigail's gone," one of the girls spoke up.

Christine felt her stomach drop.

"What?"

"She's not in her bed," the same voice said.

"No..." Christine choked, rushing to Abigail's bunk.

Sure enough, the bed was empty.

"I'm sure she's fine," Harper said. "She's probably in the restroom."

Even though Christine knew she wasn't, she dashed into the bathroom to check anyway.

No sign of Abigail.

"She's not there." Christine was so distraught she could barely get the words out. Then, without waiting for Harper's response, she burst out the front door of the cabin and screamed into the night air, "ABIGAIL!"

"Christine!" Harper hissed, darting after her. "Calm down!"

"I can't. She's gone. I don't know where she - " And that's when Christine broke down sobbing.

"Shh..." Harper pulled her friend into her arms and held her. "Listen to me. We're going to find her, all right? But you need to pull yourself together."

She was right. Christine wouldn't be of any help to anyone when she was so upset she couldn't think straight.

"Wh - what do we do?" she stammered through her tears.

"First, we're going to do a thorough check of the cabin. She could still be in the closet, under one of the beds, maybe even in our bathroom. If we don't find her, we're going to radio Tracy, Julie, Kip, everyone. Then we'll organize a search and rescue. But you've got to keep it together. Not just for Abigail, but for the rest of the girls. Do you think you can do that?"

"Yes," Christine answered, her voice trembling.

"Good," Harper said. "Now let's go find her."

They didn't.

They searched all night. When they didn't find her in the cabin, they issued a Code Amber, alerting their fellow counselors and the rest of the camp staff to Abigail's absence. Together, they searched the campgrounds until sunrise, but they found neither hide nor hair of the missing girl.

Before breakfast, Julie and Tracy called for an emergency camp assembly in the dining hall.

"I'm sure most of you have heard by now that Abigail Murphy disappeared last night," Tracy announced. "We want you to know that we are doing everything we can to find her. We've contacted the local authorities and they'll be arriving soon to aid in the search. In the meantime, we want all of you to stay together, so you're going to be spending the day in the activity center. At least until Abigail is found."

Christine fought back tears as she observed the distraught and confused looks on the faces of their campers.

This wasn't how it was supposed to be. Their week at camp should have been the best week of their summer. Now their memories would be tainted with feelings of fear and a doubles dose of a reality they were far too young to have to experience.

And Abigail... Sweet little Abigail... Out there in the unknown, alone and frightened. Or worse...

No. No. Christine wouldn't accept that. She couldn't. Abigail *had* to be out there. She *had* to be okay.

But *where?*

They'd searched everywhere; the cabins, the health center, the boathouse. They'd combed every inch of every trail, but there was no sign she'd ever even set foot in the woods. It was like she'd vanished into thin air.

Christine sighed and glanced out the window, catching a glimpse of her haggard reflection in the glass.

Reflection...

Abigail's reflection.

Her mirror image.

The mirror.

It was a long shot. Christine knew that. But it was the one place they hadn't thought to look. Or perhaps, more accurately, that they hadn't *known* to look.

"Christine?" Kip whispered, taking her hand. "Are you okay?"

"I think I might know where to find her," she answered.

Then, without another word, she bolted out of the dining hall and into the woods.

"Christine! Wait!" Kip called after her.

But she didn't slow down. She ran until her legs were aching and sweat was rolling down her neck. Even when her lungs began to strain for air, she kept pushing forward until finally, *finally*, she passed the large oak tree between Cabin 3B and the archery range. The one with the trail markers.

She was close.

Just a few more paces...

There.

The mirror was still there.

And standing there, still dressed in her pink and white nightgown, was Abigail.

"Abigail!" Christine cried out, weak with joyful relief.

The little girl didn't respond. The mirror had her transfixed again.

"Abigail," Christine repeated gently, reaching out for the girl's shoulder. "Are you all right? We've been looking everywhere for - "

But the words died on her lips when Abigail turned to face her.

To Christine's horror, the thing standing in front of the mirror wasn't Abigail at all, but a monster, with sharp, twisted features, glowing red eyes, and a mouth that stretched into a wide, gruesome smile.

"Christine? Where are you?"

She heard Kip calling her name, but she couldn't answer. She wanted to scream... wanted to run... but she was frozen to the spot, staring into the eyes of the evil entity.

"Christine!"

Now Kip's voice was right behind her, but strange power of Abigail's doppelgänger still held her captive.

It wasn't until he reached out and touched her that the spell was broken.

Frantic with fear, Christine turned wide, terrified eyes on Kip.

"What happened? Are you okay?" Kip asked her. It was like he couldn't even see the specter standing before them.

"It's Abigail! Don't you see - "

But when Christine looked back, the doppelgänger had vanished.

All that remained was the broken mirror, and in it, her own monstrous reflection.

Forsaken Mirror
In the woods

Do not look me in the eye
For if my reflection
Perchance you see,
Then surely you will die.

Writers' Retreat

When I was in eighth grade, my science class took a field trip to NASA to learn about the space program. Our guide, a former astronaut named Kristen, gave us a brief history of their most successful missions and what it would take to qualify to fly if we ourselves dreamt of one day traveling to the stars. Back then, you had to be in prime physical shape if you wanted to be an astronaut. A four-eyed fourteen-year-old with a crooked spine and trick knees didn't stand a chance.

Things are different today. Now, if you want to take a spin around the moon or a weekend getaway to Mars, all you need is a valid passport and a couple thousand extra dollars in your bank account.

Or in our case, a fancy group coupon.

I'm not going to lie to you. The prices that we're paying for this little excursion are still out of this world, but they're not nearly as high as we would be paying solo. Of course, if we were going this alone, I wouldn't be going at all. This whole trip was William's idea.

William Curry is my mentor and head of our small writer's group based in Denison, Texas. Together, we make up a company of exactly eight. Ken the historian. Vince the adventurer. Owen the dreamer. Hannah and Val, the sci-fi sisters. William, our fearless leader. Armande, William's wife and our voice of reason. And then there's me: Alexandra the hopeless romantic.

Make that the hopeless romantic who really likes keeping her feet on the ground. You know, on Earth. Where there are trees and mountains and oceans. And my cat.

Do they even have cats on Mars? Probably not. But you know, I guess I'll find out when we arrive in just four short days.

God, I can't believe this. How can this be real? I'm going to Mars. How many people have fantasized about walking the red planet or watching the sun rise over those dusty craters? Too many to count, I'd wager. And yet, here I am, about to live the lifelong dream of hundreds of thousands... and absolutely dreading the very idea.

To the rest of my group, this is the chance of a lifetime, an actual sci-fi fairy tale come to life. Especially William. He is so excited. He and Armande are actually financing the better part of our voyage. Last year, William's long-lost aunt (yes, for real) passed away and left him a literal fortune. And the very first thing he did was book eight round-trip tickets to Mars. When he invited us along, he told us to think of it as our very first writers' retreat.

Let me tell you, this is one humdinger of a retreat. I would have been happy with a cabin in Colorado or a camping trip to Arkansas. But William doesn't believe in missed opportunities or in living within the limits. Of anything. Including our atmosphere.

It probably wasn't his aunt's best decision, entrusting William J. Curry with a lot of money. But oh well. The damage has been done.

I just hope it doesn't leave me stranded on a strange world thirty-four million miles from the only planet I'll ever call home.

It's the morning of the launch and I'm frenzied and exhausted at the same time. I was up half the night trying to figure out what to pack for two weeks of red dust storms or solar winds or whatever the weather happens to be beneath the biosphere they've constructed for human habitation on Mars. I checked the website for the Aresian Resort where we'll be staying (yes, Mars has a resort and yes, that resort has a website) and it just says to "Come as you are! There's something for everybody at the Galaxy's Favorite Getaway!" The weirdest thing about this website is that there are hardly any pictures of what this place actually looks like. Sure, there are a few shots of tourists exploring craters and skiing around the polar ice caps, but none of the actual resort. From what I've read, that's on purpose. The people who run the Aresian really want their visitors to be surprised when they arrive. On the one hand, that's kind of cool. On the other, it's kind of terrifying.

I literally have no idea what to expect from this journey. What if we get there and the resort isn't a resort at all? What if it's just a bunch of dwell-able caves carved into the side of a canyon? Or some weird Martian laboratory that's full of creepy space robots?

I do not like robots. At all.

"All right! We are all here and ready to go!" William grins as Vince, late as usual, drags his carry-on luggage to our little corner where we've convened.

The spaceport is a lot like a smaller version of an airport, but with newer technology, brighter lights, and cleaner floors. Also, everyone is running around in a designer spacesuit. William's is red and it has some symbol from *Star Trek* on it because of course it does. Armande's is purple. Very purple. Me? I got the cheapest suit I could find. It's plain old white and has an embroidered emblem of what, for some reason, I thought was an armadillo but is actually a weird little alien head. I'm really hoping Mars' permanent residents don't find it offensive. Even though I do think those people are just absolutely out of their minds.

Why would anyone want to live on Mars? I mean, yeah, thanks to modern technology, home is only a short three-day journey away, but I can't imagine the day-to-day life on Mars is what you'd call high quality. Sure, they've got great Wi-Fi but I know for a fact there are no movie theaters or Super

Targets there. No gardens. No blue skies or fields of sunflowers. Just dust and craters and an eerie orange sky.

What if we get hit by a meteor? Does Mars have meteor warnings?

"Now, we still have about an hour to go before we board. Does anyone have any last-minute questions? Ideas? What about your goals? What is everyone hoping to get out of this retreat?" William wants to know.

The answers are what you'd typically expect from a writers' group. Owen wants to finish the novel he's been working on since he was sixteen. Hannah and Val want to get a real feel for what it's like to live on a different planet. Vince is hoping to improve his poetry.

I guess aside from simply surviving this trip, I'm hoping for inspiration. I've always loved books and I've always dreamed of writing one. I must have at least a dozen half-written first chapters saved to my computer, but for some reason, I've never been able to commit to any of them. I'm hoping that this experience changes that. Or at least helps me discover whatever it is I'm missing.

"What about you, William? What are you hoping for?" Ken asks.

"I want this journey to change all of our lives!" William exclaims. I swear, he's like a jovial wizard in a Disney cartoon. "And I know it will! I can feel it!"

I can feel it, too.

I can feel it as I'm trying not to pass out as our starship engines fire up and prepare to blast us into outer space.

Don't throw up. Don't throw up. Stay conscious. Take deep breaths. And again, please, please, please don't throw up.

In spite of my general sense of unease and impending doom, this actually is a pretty great ship. It's actually kind of like a flying hotel. Our cabins are comfortable, the food isn't dry or frozen, and it makes its own artificial gravity so we don't have to worry about floating up out of our seats as we gather in the common area to mingle or read or watch the evening news.

Unfortunately, all of the artificial gravity in the world isn't enough to keep my early-morning breakfast burritos settled in my stomach. Just as the brilliant blue sky outside my window fades to a vast and endless black, I retch my guts out into the surprisingly low-tech barf bag I've been clutching since the second I fastened my seatbelt.

So much for an inspirational experience.

"You going to be okay?" Armande asks, rubbing my shoulder.

"... Doubtful..." I whimper as I heave again.

"If it makes you feel better, Owen's looking a little green around the gills, too. And he's actually excited about this trip."

I love my relationship with Armande. We're always very frank with each other. Neither of us ever feels the need to beat around the bush. And neither of us were thrilled about the idea of leaving our planet.

"Trust me, this was all William's idea," she confessed to me the night that the trip was first announced. "If I had any say in it, we'd be going to Orlando."

"If I don't make it back, will you tell my cat that I loved her?" I ask Armande. That actually gets a giggle out of her.

"Glad that you still have your wits about you."

"No. I'm about to puke my wits up. Along with my will to live."

"Just think about all the incredible things you're going to have to write about."

"Like vomiting?"

"Now you're just trying to be cynical."

"No, it's coming pretty naturally. Like the vomiting."

And with that, she laughs again. Even I manage a pathetic chuckle.

"I know you don't believe it now, but I think you're going to be happy you came," Armande says.

That's what my parents told me. And my best friends. And my therapist. And my reverend. Everyone encouraged me to go, insisted I would regret it if I didn't. After all, a writers' retreat on Mars is kind of a once in a lifetime opportunity.

The funny thing is I didn't get even half that kind of support when I started telling people that I wanted to be a writer. In fact, most of the people I told discouraged me.

"You'll never make any money."

"Why would you want to waste your time like that?"

"No, I meant what do want to do for an actual job?"

But tell people you're going on a writers' retreat to Mars and suddenly they can't get you off the planet fast enough. Go figure.

It takes me seventy-two hours, but I finally find my space legs.

Of course, since we're scheduled to land in just a few short hours, this is not the victory that it could have been. But at least now when I take my first steps on Mars, I won't be sprinting to the nearest space toilet.

The landing itself is smooth. Much smoother, in fact, than the landings I'm used to back on Earth. Instead of skidding to a stop on a runway, we float gently down through a thick haze of golden orange clouds until Mars itself finally comes into view.

The spaceport here is similar to the one back home: a shiny, sterile building with little color and even less character. But we arrive safely and that's really all that matters.

Setting foot on the ground for the first time is a surreal experience. I'm used to the thrill of touching down in a different state and knowing that I'm somewhere new. That's all too familiar. But this? This is a completely different world. And a bit to my surprise, I find myself eager to get out and see exactly what all it has to offer.

Instead of cars and highways, all of Mars is connected by an intricate series of trains that travel at breakneck speed. I'm not going to lie to you, it's kind of hard not to feel like we're living in a dystopian novel what with the high-tech transportation and the eerie landscape outside my window.

I swear, if I see anything that looks even remotely like an alien, I am hightailing it back to Earth on the quickest rocket that can carry me there.

Although I suppose that here, we're the aliens. That's a little strange to think. Maybe that's what I should write my story about. A poor society of Martians are going about their day, minding their own business, when strange aliens from the green and blue planet invade. And, you know, start building luxury resorts. But perhaps what we consider luxury, the native Martians perceive as torture. That is, until one curious Martian sneaks into the resort and discovers the wonder that is the day spa.

"I can already see my story coming to life," Hannah sighs, watching the dusty terrain pass by. "In a post-apocalyptic era, a small group of survivors flees Earth to settle on a recently discovered planet. Among them is a young heiress who grew up with everything she could possibly want but now, she's forced to live and work with those she used to look down on."

"On whom she used to look down," Vince corrects her.

"You know that never makes anyone any friends, right?" Armande asks him.

"But it's grammatically correct!" Vince argues.

"Yeah, well, so is your face," Hannah quips.

"That makes no sense at all!"

"I like that this is the first real conversation we're having on Mars," Owen laughs. "We could be marveling at the craters or imagining just how clearly we'll be able to see the stars, but no. We're talking about grammar."

"Writers are weird," Val mutters.

"I think you mean awesome!" Vince exclaims.

"No, I definitely mean weird."

"I'll drink to that," I comment. "Wait. Do they have alcohol on Mars?"

"And if they do, what's the age limit? Am I old enough to drink here?" Nineteen-year-old Owen wants to know.

"Aw, come on, now. We don't need alcohol! We're on the adventure of a lifetime!" William exclaims.

For the record, William is the only writer I've ever met who doesn't drink. Not a drop. Not even for special occasions. On the one hand, I truly admire him. On the other, I think he's totally insane.

Then again... I think to myself once I lay eyes on the Aresian Resort for the first time. Maybe William has a point.

Who needs alcohol? Seriously? This place is fantastic! This is phenomenal! There are palm trees here! Actual living, breathing palm trees! How did they get palm trees to grow on Mars? I can't even get them to grow in Dallas! I guess it must be the controlled atmosphere inside the bio-dome.

The building itself is every science-fiction lover's fantasy come to life: a shining assembly of discs and dancing spheres, sparkling with white and silver starlight, and yet adorned with so many lush bouquets of tropical flowers that even the most reluctant Earthling would find themselves feeling at home.

For our week-long stay, William has reserved an entire wing of the resort just for the eight of us. We each get our own room and the common area, where we'll meet each morning and each evening to plan our days and of course, to get some writing done, has a glass ceiling so we can gaze up and watch the galaxies at night.

"You know what's incredible?" Ken asks. "From here, the Earth is going to look like one of those distant stars."

"It certainly puts things in perspective," Hannah sighs.

"Yeah," Val agrees. "I feel so small out here."

"Really? I feel infinite and empowered," Vince declares. "I'm no longer bound to what we once believed to be rules and restrictions. The universe is ours."

Okay, I am now convinced that there is alcohol on Mars and that Vince found it.

"What about you, Alexandra?" William asks me. "What are you feeling?"

"Overwhelmed," I admit. "I don't think it's fully sunk in that this is real, that we're really here." If I'm being honest, I have no idea how William expects any of us will get any writing done. There's too much to take in! Too much to experience!

Then again, how cool would it be to be able to tell people that you wrote a book on Mars? Granted, whatever I write is going to be full of romantic sighs and stolen kisses, probably in a medieval castle and with absolutely no mention of the Red Planet... or any planet for that matter. But still.

Since we're all exhausted from our journey, we decide to take the evening to unwind, shower, relax, and write. One of the coolest things that I've learned about Mars so far is that the days here are only about forty minutes longer than our days on Earth. Good news for those of us who may be prone to jet lag.

After we've all showered and changed, we reconvene back in the common area with our computers and notebooks. I've just settled in with my pen and paper when the door leading out to the hall opens and, to my sheer and utter horror, a shiny silver robot rolls in.

"Oh God... Oh God!" I yelp and leap up onto the couch.

"Welcome," the triangular being beeps. "I am Marsha, your hostess, your housekeeper, and your friend."

No, no, no, no, no. Robots are not friends. I am not okay with this. What if it has access to our rooms? What if it decides to break in in the middle of the night and watch us sleep?

Of course, all of my friends think that Marsha is just oh, so charming.

"How very nice to meet you, Marsha," William greets it.

"Marsha! Like Mars-sha! Get it?" Owen exclaims.

"We all get it, Owen," Vince deadpans.

"Oh, this is so not cool," I mutter under my breath.

"She is a little creepy," Armande agrees. At least I have one ally.

"I am here to serve you," Marsha continues. "If you have any requests, questions, or concerns, please do not hesitate to ask."

Okay, so the good news is I don't think Marsha is a sentient robot. I think it's a highly sophisticated computer that knows just enough to be helpful. But there is still no way in Martian hell that I am ever letting it into my room.

"I've got a question for you, Marsha. What's the weather like outside?" Ken asks.

"Temperatures outside the Aresian Resort are minus 54 degrees Celsius and falling," Marsha answers.

"Ooh, chilly. We should make ourselves some hot chocolate," Ken grins.

"Would you like me to make you some hot chocolate?" Marsha asks.

"Yes. Thank you, Marsha," William says in all earnest.

"It is my pleasure," Marsha replies before rolling out of the room.

"Oh my God, that thing is going to murder all of us," I remark.

"Alex, I think you're being a little over-dramatic," Hannah tells me.

"Yeah! I like Marsha. I think she's cute," Val says.

"You know she's probably not the only robot here," Vince smirks at me. It's an evil smirk, too. "I bet she has a whole fleet of brothers and sisters. Mark. Martin. Marshall. Margaret..."

"That's great. Thank you for that." I glower at him. I swear, Vince is the older brother I never wanted.

It probably goes without saying that I get absolutely no writing done. I'm far too busy glancing over my shoulder every other second for killer robots. Granted, our killer robot did make us some ridiculously delicious hot chocolate. But that still doesn't mean I trust it.

The next morning, I rise with the pale Martian dawn. The new sun paints the hazy clouds a stunning lavender and the miles and miles of red dust glow a rusty gold. I would take a picture but I truly don't believe a pixelated image would do it justice.

Since I'm not about to call Marsha and ask it to bring me breakfast in bed, I climb out of bed, pull on a sweatshirt and a pair of jeans, and wander down to the lobby. Now that I've gotten a good night's rest, I'm noticing more and more about the Aresian Resort. For example, the hallway is lined with statues and images of Greek and Roman gods and goddesses. The gift shop actually sells a shirt that reads, *My parents went to Mars and all I got was this stupid T-shirt*. And there's an exceptionally cute guy kneeling down a mere ten feet in front of me.

I'm not ashamed to admit that the sight of him stops me dead in my tracks. Where did he even come from? I mean, I'm assuming he's from Earth. But how did I manage to miss him yesterday?

He doesn't look very tall, but he's sturdy; broad shoulders and really nice biceps. His wavy brown hair falls into intelligent eyes which are fixed and focused on -

Oh, no.

It's a robot.

He's fixing a robot.

I don't mean to gasp, but I do. And of course, he hears me and glances up.

"I'm sorry," I apologize immediately.

"No, no, it's fine. Are you all right?" Oh my God. He's British. I am about to swoon on the spot.

"Yeah. No, I'm fine. I'm great," I ramble.

"Is there anything I can help you with?" he asks.

"Oh, no. I was just... um..." What am I doing? Strolling? Spying? Thankfully, the sweet smell of coffee wafting through the air reminds me that I'm looking for food. Specifically, breakfast food. Do they have chickens on Mars? If not, how do they get the eggs here? Finally, I answer my handsome stranger, "I was looking for the dining room."

"It's just right through there." He points to two glass doors. "But you know, Marsha could have easily served you from your room."

"Yes. I am happy to be of service," the broken Marsha chimes in. I grimace and take an automatic step back. Cute Robot Guy laughs.

"Not keen on robots, are you?"

"Not particularly, no." I try to keep my tone as nonchalant as possible.

"Guess I'm the last guy who should be hoping to make your acquaintance then," he smiles. Then, rising to his feet, he holds out a large hand. "I'm Jack."

"Alexandra," I introduce myself.

"Lovely name."

"Thank you," I blush. I definitely wasn't expecting to meet any guys during my stay on Mars. Especially any as cute as Jack. "So uh... are you like a robot mechanic or something?"

"Actually, I'm an engineer. I helped design all of the Marshas you meet here at the Aresian."

So I've just insulted his life's work. Perfect.

"Oh, wow. That's incredible," I tell him. "I'm sorry that I... uh... didn't seem very appreciative."

"It's all right. Believe me, you're not the first guest to shy away from her."

"I'm not?"

"Last month, a woman actually kicked her Marsha. Thankfully, she didn't do her any real damage. Marsha's feelings were hurt a bit, though."

I can feel my face fall.

"Are you... Do you mean... What...?"

"Don't worry, I'm joking," Jack assures me with a cheeky grin. I heave a tremendous sigh of relief. "So, it isn't necessarily the idea of a robot that concerns you. It's the idea of a robot with a sense of self-awareness and cognition."

"That is literally one of my worst nightmares," I admit.

"Mine too. So we do have something in common."

"I guess we do."

"So, Alexandra, what brings you to this side of the galaxy?" he asks.

"I'm on a writer's retreat."

Jack gives a cute little shake of his head. I guess that wasn't what he was expecting.

"I've got to tell you, that's a new one," he says.

"You mean that's not why most people fly to Mars?" I laugh.

"I'd say the majority are here on research grants. The rest are fulfilling a lifelong dream. But I don't think many of them came here to write."

"Well, I will tell you that this is a lifelong dream for most of my group."

"But not for you?" Jack asks.

"I'm more of a white sand and suntan kind of girl."

"Fair enough."

Just then, Marsha beeps, interrupting what I'm all but certain was about to be a magical moment.

Have I mentioned that I hate robots?

"I should probably get back to work. It was a pleasure to meet you, Alexandra."

"Likewise," I tell him. "Maybe I'll see you around."

"I'll be here."

I'm going to go ahead and take that as a date.

I don't tell anyone about Jack, mostly because I don't want anyone to know I'm shallow enough to think that a cute British guy is the single most interesting thing about visiting a different planet. I should be far more taken with the opportunities to see, experience, and explore, but if I'm being totally honest with myself, my thoughts keep drifting back to Jack. But in my defense, I am a romance author. Or at least, I will be once I actually write my romance novel. Maybe Jack will be my inspiration...

"Eh-hem," Armande clears her throat, snapping me out of my infatuation-induced stupor.

"What?" I ask.

"Crater-jumping. Are you in?" Hannah asks.

"Oh... uh... sure. Sounds fun." Fun. Dangerous. Tomayto, tomahto. "When are we going?"

"First thing tomorrow morning," William answers.

"Cool. I'm in."

"So what were you thinking about so intently?" Vince asks. Of course he'd be the one to call me out.

"Nothing."

"Uh-huh. Right."

Thankfully, William changes the subject before Vince can interrogate me further.

"So, how is everybody doing? Has anyone gotten any writing done?"

"I've been doing some outlining but I've also been learning a lot about the planet," Ken answers. "Did you know that there's a library dedicated exclusively to the history and study of Mars? It's right here at the resort."

"I did not know that," William answers.

"We've already got our character list, a timeline, and we even created a soundtrack on our tablet," Val declares.

"I haven't written anything yet, but I've been doing a lot of reading," Owen says.

"That's just as important," William says.

"How about you, Daydream Sally?" Vince asks. I'm assuming he means me.

"I've got a few ideas," I answer lightly.

"Oh yeah? Care to share?"

"Eventually."

I'm going to have to do a little more research first. And by that, I mean I'm going to have to spend a little more time with a certain handsome space engineer.

I get my opportunity after we return from crater-jumping, which was actually a lot more fun than I thought it'd be. Of course, we had to be in our space suits, but the thrill of exploring an actual Martian crater far outweighed the embarrassment I felt once again donning that tacky outfit.

Thankfully, I'm able to shower and change into a summer skirt and tank top before I set out to "accidentally" run into Jack again. I even take my notebook and half a dozen colored pens to make it look like I actually plan on writing.

I find him in the library that Ken mentioned yesterday. He's sitting at a computer and oh, be still my heart, he's wearing glasses. As if he couldn't get any cuter.

"Oh. Hey, Jack," I greet him like I'm surprised. He looks up and me and smiles.

"Alexandra. Hello. My, what a small world."

"Smaller than Earth," I quip and take a seat next to him.

"This is true," he acknowledges. "So, how are you? Are you enjoying your stay?"

"Yeah, it's great. I got to go crater-jumping this morning."

"You know, I still haven't found time to make it out there."

"Are you serious?" I ask. "But you live here."

"I spend all my time working."

"Well, that's no fun."

He shrugs.

"This is a dream come true for me, but it's also a very coveted position. I have to work hard because there are literally thousands of engineers back on Earth waiting with baited breath to take my place."

"Oh. I guess I never thought of that." Suddenly, I'm embarrassed. "I should stop distracting you, then."

"No. Please. You're a welcome distraction," he assures me. "Besides, I've gotten rather good at working and talking at the same time."

"Sadly, I cannot say the same," I admit.

"So, what are you writing about?"

"I'm still trying to figure that out. Do you have any suggestions?"

"Well, I'm no storyteller, but a trip to Mars seems like kind of a cool idea."

"Yeah, but isn't it a bit overdone?" I tease. "What about you? What's your story?"

"I'm afraid it's rather a dull one," he warns me.

"You live on Mars. Come on, that's way more interesting than all the Earth guys can boast."

"I suppose that's true. But I wasn't exaggerating when I told you that I spend all my time working. That applied back when I was still living on Earth. I wanted this so badly that I let it consume me. Don't get me wrong, I have no regrets. I'm proud of where I am and I love what I do. It just doesn't make for much of a story."

"Oh, but see, that's where you're wrong. I think it's fascinating that this is the path you chose."

"And why is that?"

"Probably because I don't understand it. Mars, so far, really is wonderful. Much better than I expected it to be. But I've only been away for five days and I already miss Earth."

"I miss it too, on occasion. But thanks to modern technology, I'm able to video chat with my family whenever I want."

"And you can visit."

"If I can get the time off."

"So why did you choose to come here?" I ask.

"Like I said, it was all I ever wanted. I grew up dreaming of being an astronaut, of walking on the moon. Then, when I was in Year 7, I found out about the engineers and scientists working around the clock to make Mars inhabitable for us. I was already a bit of a weird kid on Earth. I didn't make friends easily. I figured I didn't have all that much to lose, but I had a whole new world to gain."

"And is it everything you dreamed it would be?"

"Almost," he answers. "It's still not very easy to make friends."

"I'll be your friend," I offer. Of course, I'll be gone in less than a week, which doesn't make for a very promising friendship. It makes for an even less promising romance.

And even though he is also well aware of this, he smiles.

"Yeah?"

"Yeah. You know, as long as you keep your creepy robots away from me."

With that, he throws his head back and laughs.

"It's a deal."

As much as I enjoy spending time with Jack, keeping a new friendship a secret from your tight-knit group of other friends is something of a challenge. Particularly when the new friend in question is intelligent, funny, kind... basically everything I've ever wanted in a guy. What a cruel trick of fate.

I finally find the man of my dreams and his dreams led him to a life on Mars.

And okay, I probably haven't known him long enough to be calling him the man of my dreams. But the more I get to know him, the more I dread the idea of saying goodbye to him.

I'm trying not to think about that now, as I sit with him beneath the open glass ceiling of the resort's stargazing deck. Technically, I think it's called an observation deck, but that doesn't sound nearly as romantic.

"So have you started writing yet?" Jack asks.

"A little bit. This and that, here and there." That's a bold-faced lie. I haven't written a word.

"Are you happy with it?"

"Too soon to tell."

"You know, you still haven't told me your story. Why do you want to be a writer?"

"I've always loved to read. I love that books can take me anywhere. I love that my favorite characters actually feel like friends. And I love that stories give me hope... even on the darkest days."

Jack doesn't say anything for a moment. He just stares at me with beautiful hazel eyes.

"I have a confession to make," he finally says. "I don't read very much fiction. In fact, I think the last novel I read was for an assignment at University. But the way your eyes lit up just now... you make me wonder exactly what I've been missing."

"You know, you make me wonder the same thing."

He almost kisses me then. I think he would have, too, had William and Armande not chosen that precise moment to appear out on the deck.

"Well, well. What have we here?" Armande asks, crossing her arms over her chest.

"Oh... Uh... Hey, y'all." I greet them nervously.

"What exactly is going on out here?"

"Nothing. You know. Just talking."

Armande doesn't buy that for a second.

"Right. And who are you?"

"This is my friend, Jack. He's an engineer and inventor here at the Aresian," I introduce him. "Jack, this is my mentor, William, and his wife, Armande."

"Ah. More writers. It's a pleasure," Jack says, standing up to shake their hands.

"And why haven't we heard anything about you?" Armande wants to know.

"Afraid I can't answer that one," Jack tells her.

That's when all eyes turn to me.

"Uh... Well... You know..."

"You didn't want us knowing you were sneaking around with a boy when you were supposed to be writing?" Have I ever mentioned that Armande isn't one to beat around the bush? Because she isn't. She cuts straight to the chase. Every. Time.

William, on the other hand, is all kinds of intrigued by Jack.

"So, are you really an inventor? And you live here? You've got to tell me what that's like. What all have you invented? How long did you have to study to qualify?"

"William, honey, give the boy a break," Armande intervenes.

"I'm sorry. I can't help it. I have so many questions. What's it like to really live here? Do you think you'll ever move back to Earth?"

I can't pretend I haven't thought of asking him that question myself. But I haven't managed to conjure up the courage. Not because I'm embarrassed to ask, but because I'm not sure my heart could handle the answer.

"I've considered it," Jack says. "Maybe in a few years. Right now, I'm in the middle of three major projects and I've got ideas for at least two more."

"And you couldn't work on them from Earth?"

"Not these particular projects, no. Unfortunately."
That's when Jack glances back to catch my eye.

"Ah. I see," William says. "Well, this is an incredible opportunity for you. And what a work environment!"

"Yeah. It's not too shabby," Jack grins. "Though I'll admit I've recently become aware of its shortcomings." Again, he looks at me. I can feel my heart skip more than a couple beats.

"Well, take solace in the fact that what's meant to be will be," William grins. That's easy for him to say. He and Armande have been together since they met in college. I'm thirty, ridiculously single, and two days away from leaving the only guy I've ever felt really crazy about on Mars. If this is what's meant to be, the universe has a bizarre sense of humor.

But Jack just nods. Then, shoving his hands into the pockets of his well-worn jeans, he says, "It's getting late. I should probably say goodnight."

God, how I wish he wouldn't.

But I don't argue with him. I simply bid him goodnight and follow William and Armande back to our wing of the resort.

"Are you okay?" William asks me.

"Yeah. Why?"

"I know your heart. And I can tell that you really like him."

"I do," I answer with a shrug. "But I also know that long distance relationships are hard enough when you're in different cities. How am I supposed to make one work with a guy who lives halfway across the solar system?"

"You never know," William says.

"Well, I think you're being smart," Armande tells me. "Have fun getting to know him. Enjoy his company. But don't put your life on hold for him."

"But stay in touch with him. If you want," William advises.

"I'd like to. I hope to," I tell them.

"Then do."

Our adventure on Mars ends with an exhilarating round of buggy racing. I had no idea this was even a thing, but Vince and Owen somehow found out about it and convinced William that it was something that we needed to experience.

Actually, they didn't have to convince William at all. It was Armande and I who were the skeptics. But just like every other chance I've taken during my stay here, space-racing across Mars' wide red terrain is definitely worth it.

It's especially worth it because Jack is able to come along.

"I can't believe I've been here for a year and a half and never experienced that," he laughs once we're safely back inside the resort.

"I can't believe you've been here for a year and a half." I've only been here a week and it feels like a lifetime.

Then, the laughter on his face melts away and he adopts a more somber expression.

"I can't believe you're leaving in just a few hours," he murmurs.

"I can't believe I didn't want to come at all."

And finally, finally, he pulls me into his arms as I wrap my arms around his neck and kiss him. Maybe I'm still on a high from buggy racing, or maybe it's due to the fact that I'm already lighter on Mars than I am on Earth, but Jack's kiss leaves me feeling weightless, breathless, and dizzy. I'm ecstatic, euphoric, and even though my eyes are closed, I am well aware of every star shining in the galaxies above us.

Then again, I realize, gazing into those beautiful hazel eyes, perhaps it has nothing to do with Mars and everything to do with him.

I know, standing here in his arms, that I may very well never see him again. Our story may be one of star-crossed lovers rather than a match made in the heavens. But I suppose that's the beautiful thing about stories. There's never a guarantee that they'll work out the way you want them to, but there is always that possibility.

And maybe, while I wait to find out how our story will end, I'll write one of my own.

The Water's Edge

I died at sea.

The ship that was supposed to be taking me home capsized and sank just a few miles off shore from our small fishing village. Several managed to save themselves. They found refuge in the lifeboats or on bits of floating debris. Some may have even tried to swim for it.

The rest of us slipped down into the depths with the ship, fading out of the life that we knew and into the darkness of the icy black ocean. Our bodies were never found; our loved ones left to wonder.

I may have had a family once. A mother, father, sister, perhaps even a lover. But if I had, they have since been forgotten. All memories of them washed away like sand on the shoreline and replaced by images of lightning, sea monsters, and shipwrecks. A long and haunted nightmare.

That's what becomes of us. There is no peace, no paradise, no glimpse of pure and heavenly light. Only the vast and bitter emptiness of death and a cold, gray ocean. And the fear. Always the fear. Death is a frightening experience. Every nerve, every instinct, every living fiber is designed to fight it. A body's desire to keep itself alive is powerful, but death is overwhelming, all-consuming, and in the end, it always wins. Even those who still live walk in the knowledge that death is waiting for them. It's only a matter of time.

For many, death waits until their hair has gone white, their skin, pale and wrinkly with age. But others are not so fortunate. Many will die of illness or injury well before their time. Others will be lost in tragic accidents or perhaps even by the hand of another. I don't know what becomes of them. All I know is what awaits those taken by the sea.

We are not ghosts, per se, for we are no longer entirely human. Instead, in the days, months, years following our demise, our souls merge with the spirit of the sea. We become the rolling fog that blinds and disorients, the riptides that seize and capture, the voices on the wind that beckon sailors to watery graves. We are the fears and doubts and hesitations of all fishermen, seafarers, and villagers who call the waterfront home.

The town itself is rather small, with far fewer living souls than dead. There is a market, a church, and, of course, the boat docks, to which I am often particularly drawn. I cannot say why. Perhaps it is a small piece of my living self being called back to a place I once loved or the vibrant colors of the small fishing vessels. Or perhaps it means nothing at all.

The villagers' houses are all similar: white, modest buildings with black roofs, doors, and shutters. In recent years, the residents have constructed a barrier between the sea and the houses in the hopes of keeping the tides, as well as unwelcome spirits, at bay. The tides respect the barricade, but the spirits pass through as though it is not even there.

I never wanted to frighten the living, but in a sense, it cannot be avoided. We exist as fear and through fear. It is our purpose now, and I wish with all my being that it could be avoided. I feel that the others do as well. Still, night after night, we wander throughout the village. We are seldom seen, but never do we go unnoticed. One way or another, our presence is always made known.

For the children who are warned to stay away from the water after sunset, we are the creatures of the deep. We fill their imaginations with thoughts of monstrous eels and ravenous sharks. The ocean is a world full of the unknown, and for the boys and girls who have never ventured farther than their feet can reach, the underwater realm can be a wonderful and terrifying mystery. How are they to know whether there are sea dragons dwelling in undersea caves? Or colossal squids waiting to take them all, one by one? The stories may not all be true, but they are effective, and they stay with these fresh and innocent minds long after the lights go out.

Then there are the maidens, left alone to wait and wonder when their beloved sailors might return to them, or if, in fact, they will return at all. Their most vivid nightmares are plagued by images of their lovers gasping, drowning, being swallowed by the sea. I try to avoid these young women at all costs, for their longing and sorrow is more than even my lifeless heart is willing to endure.

I have to think now, seeing the torture and torment forced upon them, that those who do love must be mad. In what world does it make sense to care for someone so terribly that the very idea of not being with them brings the soul to ruin? While it may be true that love has the power to inspire and enlighten and enrich, it also possesses an overwhelming power to destroy. Just like the ocean.

Perhaps I have forgotten what it is like to love. Or death has robbed me of the ability. Either way, love inspires a fear in living souls to rival only death itself. If there is one thing that mortals fear above their own death, it is the potential death of someone they love.

Some in the village are lucky enough to be alone in the world. The lighthouse keeper, for example. I visit him often, usually on stormy nights when the forces of violent wind and wave threaten the very foundation of the village. He is young, no older than twenty-five, and he fears the thunder above all else. I've tried to see inside his mind, but he never lets me in, for he is almost always busy. The light demands tending, and he does his best to put his fears aside to see to his responsibilities.

I admire the lighthouse keeper. He is intriguing to me; tall and thin, with messy red hair, blue-green eyes, and a face full of freckles. He seems to be intelligent. He spends most of his spare time reading books in his armchair or studying maps at his cluttered desk. I wonder if he dreams of sailing, or if he plans to leave the village. Other nights, I have seen him sit and gaze at the fire for hours at a time, lost in his own fantasies. Those nights, he barely seems to know that I'm there. But then the thunder begins to rumble. What little color remains beneath his plethora of freckles drains from his face and he realizes he is not the only soul inside the small cottage beneath the towering light.

There are nights I leave the lighthouse keeper for a moment or two to step outside and watch the beam dance across the sky. Through mist and fog and rain, the light comes to life, and though it may sound strange, I swear that it never shines the same way twice. Like the sea itself, the light from the lighthouse is constantly changing, shifting. Perhaps it has a spirit all its own. If it does, I hope it is kinder than what I have become.

I like to think that, had I lived, I would have become acquainted with the young man who lives in the lighthouse. I believe he could tell me fascinating stories and teach me everything he has learned from his books and his studies. I know so very little in this state of existence. Fear, death, and the sea. That is all I am allowed. But what of the world I used to know? The world that the living so easily take for granted? Sometimes I glance over the lighthouse keeper's shoulder at his maps and pictures. I see images of places and things that I do not recognize, but feel I once may have known. Is it possible that I have seen forests, meadows, and mountains? I hope it is. Though I know it is too much to think I shall ever see them again.

On calmer nights, I go to see the harbormaster and his wife. They are a humble and sincere couple with no children, but they are beloved by the community. The harbormaster's wife loves to bake, and she often participates in local fairs and picnics. She also quilts. I wonder if I could have been like her one day. I don't remember what I enjoyed in life, but seeing the joy that her work brings her leads me to believe I must have had something. My life could not have been empty.

The harbormaster, like the lighthouse keeper, often sits in his armchair by the fire, but instead of reading or studying, he writes. He chronicles his entire life in an old brown journal. I cannot help thinking how wise he is and how much I wish I had done the same. In his writing, he leaves a piece of himself behind so that others may know him after he is gone. He is a man who deserves to be remembered. He spends so much of his time ensuring the safety of all who venture out to sea, and yet, he asks for nothing in return. He is a good and selfless man, one who cherishes life more than anyone I've encountered in the village.

Like so many, the harbormaster fears death, but in a way that I rarely see. He fears being responsible for death. This, of course, is absurd, for no one is responsible for death. No innocent soul can be expected to bear that burden. When death decides to strike, there is not a thing that can be done to stop it. Still, the harbormaster fears any error or carelessness on his part that will result in a preventable tragedy. I hate that the harbormaster carries this unnecessary weight on his mind and spirit, but it is not within my ability to free him. His wife brings him peace, and I am thankful for her, but even her soothing words and warm touch are not enough to rid him of his fears entirely. They will always haunt him, and therefore, so shall I.

The house to which I am almost constantly drawn, however, is one that belongs to a little girl and her fisherman father. I do not know what became of her mother. More often than not, I am inclined to believe that she died. But then there are nights, after the little girl has fallen asleep, that her father will sit at his bedroom window and stare out at the sea as though he is waiting for something or someone. I wonder if he is watching for sails to appear on the horizon, for the ship that will finally bring his love home to him.

I have spent many hours sitting with the fisherman in the moonlight, observing him, wishing I could bring him comfort instead of his cursed fear of the past and uncertainty. He is a very handsome man, tall and dark with a rough beard that covers the lower half of his weather-beaten face and piercing blue eyes, as intense and stormy as the sea itself. Strong and somber, he is a man of very few words. I only ever hear him speak to his daughter, whom he cherishes more than his own life or the life of any other.

Over the years, I have watched the girl grow from a fragile infant, pink and soft, to a bright and beautiful child of four or five. Her hair is light, but she has her father's beautiful blue eyes. She reminds me of a golden ray of sun through a cold, gray sky. If my world is one of death and darkness, hers is one of music and laughter. She knows no fear, only hope. She is the opposite of everything I know and everything that I am.

Tonight, I sit once again with her father, wishing I could speak to him. Again, he is distant, lost in memories, adrift in a sea of unanswered questions. I cannot begin to understand what drives the mortal being to love, but there is something about the fisherman that compels me to believe I may have once loved a man like him. He is damaged, but he is also strong. His spirit is hardened, but it is also kind and gentle. He has been broken, but his love for his daughter makes him whole.

As though she has been summoned by my thoughts, the girl's tiny footsteps echo down the hall. Moments later, she is standing in the doorway, her pretty little face illuminated by the glow of the candle she carries.

"Daddy," she whispers through the darkness.

"What is it, darling?" her father asks, turning to look at her.

The little girl crosses the room and climbs into his lap. Then, with a smile, she turns to look at me and then back to her father.

"She's here," she tells him.

"She is?" he asks. The little girl nods in response. "Is she wearing blue?"

"Yes. She always wears blue."

It isn't the first time the girl has seen me or described me to her father. When she first began opening up to him, I was certain he would not believe her. But he did, or if he did not, he at least pretended to believe. I dare to hope, however, that he does know I'm here, and that I care for both of them.

"What else, darling? What else do you see?" the fisherman asks.

"She's got wavy blonde hair. And she looks sad."

"Why do you think she's sad?"

"Because she can't speak. And because she's lonely. I think that's why she likes you so much."

"Why does she only come at night, I wonder?"

The way he speaks to her, in his deep, soothing voice, fills my being with a warmth I never knew I could still feel. Perhaps that is part of the reason I am so drawn to this man and his daughter. They reawaken emotions I have not experienced since before I died. A part of me almost feels human again.

"Because during the day, she has to go back home," the little girl explains.

"And where is her home?"

"The ocean. I think she is a mermaid."

It is strange to think that to the entire village, I am fear, a foul spirit, as dark and threatening as the deepest depths of the ocean. But to this girl, this pure, beautiful, precious girl, I am a creature of fantasy, her very own fairy tale. She looks at me not with fear, but with wonder and joy. How she does not see me for what I am, I cannot say, but I am grateful.

"Do you think she'll stay till sunrise?" her father asks.

The girl shakes her head.

"No. She'll be gone soon. She just wanted to see you." The girl is intuitive.

"Well, perhaps she'll come again," the fisherman says. And then, for a brief moment, he smiles.

"She will," his daughter assures him. "She always does."

An Empty Building

They say the old building comes alive at night. Not that I really know who "they" are. As far as I know, no one comes out here. Why would they? What remains here isn't even a ghost town. It's a ghost of a ghost town. Only the church still stands.

It's a simple structure: made of wood, painted white, one story, with a single steeple looming over what used to be the entrance. The windows are either shattered shards of glass or boarded up with crooked pieces of wood. In the daylight, it's actually sort of beautiful, there amidst the dying trees and an overgrowth of brown leaves, vines, and twigs. It almost looks like a scene out of a painting. But come nightfall, everything changes.

I'd never seen it personally until tonight, but I suddenly understand the whispers and myths surrounding this place. Even in the absence of moonlight, the building seems to give off a sort of glow. But it's not warm or shimmering. It's eerie, almost sinister, and yet, in a weird way, I feel that it's inviting us in. It's like it knows we're coming. It's been waiting for us.

"Okay. Let's do this," Carter hisses through the evening shadows.

"This is gonna be sick!" Elijah exclaims, shifting his video camera from one hand to the other.

"I think *I'm* gonna be sick," I mutter. I don't want to do this. Everything inside of me is telling me this is a bad idea. Even the local vandals avoid this building because they know its dark history.

"Gray, what did we say about being a whiny little bitch?" Carter demands. "Look, we all agreed we were gonna do this. You're not backing down now. Besides, it's just a building."

"If it's just a building then why are we doing this?" I argue.

"You know why. Everyone in town is pissing their pants about this church ever since that kid went all whack job out here. I'm tired of all the speculation. Either we're going to catch the devil in action, or we're going to prove once and for all, that all of the supernatural hype is nothing but bull."

A few weeks ago, a local high school student, Derek Moss, got lost driving along the back roads when his car broke down. His mother reported him missing later that night. Authorities found him the next morning, wandering around naked outside of the church, muttering to himself. When confronted, he began screaming, going on about the devil and how he lives inside the church. Then he collapsed. He hasn't spoken a word since.

The authorities figure that after being stranded in the middle of nowhere with no cell reception, Derek must have tried to walk to the nearest gas station, but he ended up at the church instead. What they can't figure out is what happened to him in between his car breaking down and being found in a deranged state the next morning. Doctors are calling it a mental breakdown.

This isn't the first time the old church has been rumored to host a demonic presence. Back in the sixties, an old woman burst into the church in the middle of a service, crying and begging for someone to heal her granddaughter. She claimed the girl had been possessed by a demon. The reverend agreed, and an exorcism was performed later that same day. Or at least, an exorcism was attempted.

If town folklore is to be believed, the casting out didn't work. Catholics claim it was because the exorcism wasn't approved by the Vatican. Others say it was because the minister was in over his head. Then there are the skeptics who claim that the girl was never possessed at all, just very sick, and that the grandmother did her a great disservice by not seeking medical attention. Whatever the reason, the exorcism went terribly wrong and the girl ended up dying there in the church.

That was the last time parishioners ever set foot inside the building.

Rumors of a dark presence spread like wildfire. Soon, nothing but fear and superstition existed within a fifty-mile radius of the church.

"So how do we get in?" Elijah asks.

"I'll check the front door. If that's sealed, we can probably climb in through a window or something," Carter answers. "Come on."

Breaking and entering. That will look great on my college application.

Our footsteps crackle through the fields of twigs and dry grass as we approach the building. Perhaps the years of spooky stories and supernatural warnings have engraved themselves in my mind, but the closer we get to the church, the more I begin to feel confined, trapped. Like the night sky is constricting and closing in around me. It's so open out here. I shouldn't be feeling this way.

Stop it. It's all in your mind. It's just a building. An empty building.

As Carter somewhat predicted, the front door is sealed shut by years of overgrowth and neglect. Elijah makes sure to linger for a moment there on the doorstep to get a shot of the old wooden cross, still hanging above the entryway.

"This is creepy as all hell, isn't it, Gray?" he asks, sounding more like a kid at an amusement park than a teenager about to break into a building supposedly haunted by the devil himself.

"It really is." I don't even try to hide my lack of enthusiasm.

I don't know why I'm so reluctant. When we first started planning this excursion a few weeks ago, I was all for it. Hell, I was the one who suggested we take a video camera along to document our findings. But as the night drew nearer, I began to feel more apprehensive, so much so that I told Carter that I wanted to back out. He wouldn't let me.

As we make our way around the side of the building, pushing back dead tree branches and stepping through a tangled web of vines and thorns, I'm overcome by the dreadful sensation that we're being watched. My head whips around to the closest window. I don't know what I'm expecting to see. A dark silhouette? A pair of glowing red eyes? But there's nothing. We forge on.

Finally, we come to a boarded-up window with a loose plank. Carter reaches into his backpack and pulls out a long, rusty crowbar. In the silence of the night, the creaking and cracking of wood and nails seem to make much more of a racket, and I'm almost afraid someone in the vicinity will hear it and call the police. Then I remember we're all alone out here. There's no one to hear it.

Once a few more boards come off, Carter says, "Okay. I'll go in first. Then, Elijah, you hand me the camera. Gray, keep an eye out."

I do as he says, watching the field and distant woods surrounding us. There's no telling what might be out there. No matter what that may be, I can't help but think it's probably friendlier than whatever might be waiting to greet us inside the old church.

After Elijah swings his long legs over the window ledge and into the church, it's my turn. I hoist myself up, careful to duck my head. The last thing any of us needs out here is a concussion or an open wound. Even if there are no demons around, there are plenty of other varmints. As my feet hit the dirty old floorboards, I can hear the faint *scritch-scritch* of insects scurrying around the crevices and corners of the building.

At first glance, nothing looks out of place. About two dozen rows of pews still stand on either side of the center aisle, though they're so covered in dust and cobwebs that they appear ghostly. The rest of the furnishings, of which there are very few, seem lost, forlorn. The very atmosphere is heavy with a tangible sorrow. Is it possible for a building to experience human emotions? Or is it all just my imagination?

"Elijah," Carter whispers. "Film me."

Elijah obliges and turns the camera on Carter.

"Well, this is it!" Carter announces, raising his arms in the air. "This is the fabled home of the devil. Now maybe it's just me, but if I were some all-powerful evil entity, this doesn't exactly look like the kind of place I'd choose to haunt. What do you think, Gray?"

Without warning, Elijah turns the camera on me.

"Oh... yeah. Right," I respond. I don't know if there's something in here with us or not, but if there is, I don't want to provoke it.

"What's the matter?" Carter demands.

"Nothing!"

"You're kidding me. You're still scared?"

"Did I say that?"

"You don't have to. It's plastered all over your pathetic face. What, Gray? You think that the big bad devil is going to come out and devour you?" He snickers. Then, he turns to face what remains of the altar and calls, "D'ja hear that, Satan? We're waiting for you! Oh, Lucifer! Any demons in the house? Olly, olly, oxen —"

Thump.

We all flinch.

"What the hell was that?" Elijah asks.

"Sounded like something hitting the floor," Carter answers. "Come on, let's investigate."

I follow, if for no other reason than there's safety in numbers.

As we seek out the source of the noise, I strain my ears for any sounds that may indicate that we're not alone in here. A rush of air. Muffled footsteps. But there's nothing. I'm almost inclined to wonder if what we heard wasn't a malicious spirit at all, just an animal, or maybe a shift in the foundation.

Then, we see it. An old book is lying face down in between the rows of pews. Carter reaches for it and mutters an expletive under his breath.

My blood runs cold when I realize exactly what he's holding.

A Bible.

But Elijah notices something different.

"Guys, look at this."

He points to a perfect rectangle, an outline of dust in the center of the pew where the book must have sat for decades. But there are no skid marks in the coating of dust. No smudges to indicate it may have been picked up or moved around. It would appear that the Bible leaped up on its own and dropped to the floor.

"Okay, this is stupid," Carter growls, dropping the Bible and wiping his hands off on his jeans. Then he straightens up and yells, "Is that all you got?"

"Carter!" I hiss.

"You serious, man?" Elijah demands.

"What? If there really is a demon in here, surely it can do a hell of a lot more than toss an old book around," Carter argues.

"Exactly. And I don't want it to," I tell him.

"Hey. This is why we came out here, remember? Evidence. Proving once and for all what does or does not exist. Now, come on."

He takes off toward the front of the church, to what used to be the altar but what now appears to be a flimsy old table, draped in a frayed and tattered white sheet. I follow closely behind Elijah, keeping an eye on the bright, glowing screen of his handheld video recorder. He's set it to night vision, and although several of the remaining windows are open enough to fill the sanctuary with natural light, it's easy to see details on the tiny screen.

"You know what's interesting?" Elijah comments. "You'd think if there was an evil spirit running around, it'd have a problem with all these crosses. There's got to be at least half a dozen."

But even as he speaks the words, I remember something my deeply religious Great Aunt Dorothy once said to me.

"A cross don't mean nothin' unless it's got the body of our crucified Lord. You understand that, Gray? A cross makes for a pretty piece of jewelry, but it is the crucifix that bears the power."

I really wish I hadn't remembered that. If I hadn't, maybe I could have found at least a little comfort in Elijah's observation.

So what, does that make me a believer now? I didn't use to be the type to believe in all this. Demons and devils are mythical creatures created to keep people in line, to scare them. That's what they've always been to me, anyway. They were stories. They were never real.

But now I'm not so sure. It's this building. It gets inside your head. The more I think about it, the less sense everything makes. Isn't this supposed to be a holy building? Dark spirits shouldn't be able to set foot here, let alone make it a home. But maybe that's a misconception too, just like the cross. Perhaps this used to be hallowed ground, but not anymore. Now it's just a building. An empty building.

"So, do you think this is where it happened?" Carter asks, pacing around the dilapidated altar.

"What? The exorcism?" Elijah asks.

"No, the Super Bowl. Of course, the exorcism!" Carter spits. "If the stories are true, that means an innocent little girl died right here in this room, possibly on this very table, because her old granny was too stupid to take her to get any real help."

And then, out of the corner of my eye, I see it. Or at least, I think I do. The dark, hunched shadow of something that doesn't look quite human slinking past one of the open windows. As soon as I turn my head, it's disappeared. But it isn't gone. There are footsteps. Only they're not footsteps. That is, they don't sound like human feet. It sounds more like the feet of some hoofed animal, walking on two legs.

"Do you hear that?" Elijah whispers.

"What the hell is that?" Carter asks.

I listen, trying to pinpoint the location of the steps, but in the old, open sanctuary, it's difficult. I can't tell if they're approaching us or if they're pacing.

"I don't know, man!" Elijah responds, using his camera to look around the room.

"Is there somebody in here with us?" Carter yells. "Show yourself!"

The room falls silent again. But something's changed. I'm beginning to feel achy, queasy. My head feels hot and stuffy like I can't force myself to concentrate or think straight. Worst of all, a horrible, putrid smell fills my nostrils and turns my already sour stomach.

"Oh, God!" Carter cries out, covering his nose and mouth with his hand.

Screeeeeech.

The shriek is piercing, unworldly, inhuman. I press my hands to my ears, but the sound still penetrates. Elijah drops to his knees. As he does, the handheld video recorder topples out of his hands and smashes into a dozen pieces.

"No!" Carter yells above the wail of the entity.

Our footage is gone. I can't believe it. The whole purpose of this excursion was to document what goes on in this building, and now it's lying in broken bits on the floor. This entire night has been for nothing.

The sanctuary falls silent again.

"Man, let's get out of here!" Elijah shudders.

I'm in agreement. With our camera gone, our footage lost, there's no point in staying.

"No! We're not going anywhere," Carter says. "That spineless ghoul is going to have to do a lot better than this if it wants us gone."

But as he speaks those words, a dreadful thought occurs to me: What if it doesn't want us gone? What if it intends a fate similar to that of Derek Moss for us? This kind of being, maybe it thrives on fear and torment. If that's the case, it wouldn't want us gone. On the contrary, it might be hell-bent on making us stay.

What if it doesn't let us leave?

I don't care what Carter says. I'm getting out of here.

Without a word, I take off running toward the nearest window. I hear Carter and Elijah shouting at me, but I ignore them as I pour every ounce of strength I have into trying to pry the window open. After a few labored moments, I feel it crack, and for one glorious second, I truly believe I've succeeded.

Then the window explodes.

I don't have time to shield my eyes from the sparkling shards of shattered glass. Several larger fragments embed themselves in my skin, but I barely feel them as a searing, white, blinding pain shoots through my right eye. I clutch my hand across my face and am horrified to feel a hot, sticky liquid oozing between my fingers. Trembling, I pull my hand away, but the darkness remains.

"Gray! Gray, are you alright, man?" I hear Elijah running up behind me. I turn to face him. He swears under his breath. "We need to get you to a hospital."

I don't have to ask him why. I can feel the piece of glass that ripped through my eyelid and planted itself in the area just above my iris. It's a pain unlike any I've ever known.

"Get it out, Elijah. Please, get it out!" I beg, frantic and utterly panicked.

"I don't think I can. We're gonna have to call an ambulance."

"No! We're *not* leaving!" Carter bellows.

"What is *wrong* with you, man? Can't you see this thing wants to hurt us?" Elijah yells back.

But Carter doesn't get the chance to answer. The invisible hoof steps are back. This time slowly pacing back and forth, like it's watching us and tapping its chin, trying to determine what it wants to do to us next.

Driving Derek Moss to the brink of insanity may have been a laugh, but here, with the three of us, this creature has the opportunity to create tension between friends, to turn us against one another.

It's playing with us before it devours us. It's enjoying this.

By now, I'm shaking so hard I can barely stand. The wound in my eye is bleeding profusely, and it's making me light-headed. My left eye is unharmed, but my vision is blurred and shaky from a combination of tears and adrenaline. It's only then that I realize... I can see it.

Perhaps it's due to the trauma or my heavily distorted vision, but it's there: a towering, behemoth of a figure, hunched over like a being that was never meant to walk on two legs. It has mangled arms and long, spindly fingers that curl out in front of its gross, hairless body. Two large, ram-like horns protrude from either side of its head. But its face, oh, its face. Death himself would be a welcome sight if it meant I never had to see that gruesome, hideous, wicked face again. Pitch black eyes that seem more like empty holes in a melted, waxy mask, a strange boar-like snout, and a mouth full of fangs that drip with rabid saliva.

I let out a cry in a voice I don't recognize. It's a guttural, feral sound; one of pure, animalistic terror. I can't find the words to describe to my companions what I'm seeing. All I know in that moment is fear.

"Gray, Gray! Calm down! It's okay!" I hear Elijah's words, but my mind cannot begin to process them. "That's it. I'm getting you out of here."

"No, stop!" Carter yells.

"To hell with you, Carter! Your friend is hurt! He might be dying! I don't know what's gotten into you but—"

All of a sudden, Elijah goes rigid and begins taking slow, deep, noisy breaths.

"Hey! What's the matter?" Carter yells.

I try to whimper something that sounds like his name, but the words die on my tongue. So I stand, watching in silent horror, as my friend's head snaps back, his eyes and mouth wide open. A few strange sounds, like tiny moans or gasps of breath, escape the back of his throat.

"Elijah!" Carter calls out.

At the sound of his name, Elijah falls forward, doubling over so that his head is in between his knees, his limp arms dangling to the floor.

"What the hell, man? Come on! Snap out of it!"

I can't support myself any longer. Feeling small and remorseful and helpless, I slink down to the floor, my back sliding against the old splintery wall, and watch through shaking fingers as Elijah, my one ally in this wretched nightmare, begins to crawl around the floor on his hands and the balls of his feet.

I think Carter is finally scared now.

With a vicious snarl, Elijah crawls over to where Carter left the Bible lying on the ground. Elijah grabs the holy book up off the floor and begins shredding it with his teeth. Then, he turns bloodthirsty eyes toward Carter.

"No! No!" Carter howls as Elijah scampers toward him.

Carter tries to leap out of the way, but Elijah takes a flying leap and tackles him. They both tumble backward onto the old altar table, which collapses and bursts into a pile of splinters and dust beneath their weight. Desperate, Carter grasps around for something, perhaps a cross or a holy relic. But there's nothing holy about this place. Not anymore. It's an empty building.

No. It's so much more than that.

My consciousness is beginning to ebb. I want to help Carter. I want to help Elijah. I should. I should help them. But I can't move my arms or my legs. Why isn't my body working?

Through a dull white haze, I see Elijah clawing Carter's neck open. I see two bloody holes where Carter's eyes used to be. I can see the inside of his mouth through a gaping wound in his cheek. If Elijah lives through this, he is going to spend the rest of his life as a murderer.

Murderer.

I'm so cold. Why can't I move?

Is this real? Or is it just a horrible nightmare? I don't know anymore. I can't think. I can't concentrate.

I just want to sleep.

The next thing I know, Elijah is crouched over me, the area surrounding his mouth and teeth stained crimson with blood.

"What to do with you?" he growls in a voice that is not his own. "Barely alive. But a waste. Such a waste. To live would be worse. So live. And wait. We will wait."

I don't know what it means. The being's speech patterns are crude, almost childlike. But I don't hear it speak again. The world around me is fading. I give up. I surrender. I close my eyes. And sleep.

A year has passed.

I live. I see with my remaining eye. I do not speak. I have not uttered a word since that night. My doctors cannot find a cause. I do not tell them. They tell me if I don't try, I will never speak again. I do not care.

Elijah was arrested. He does not remember that night at all.

Carter is dead. His funeral was held in his parents' church. I did not attend.

The devil was right. Life is worse.

After night falls, I return to my room in the hospital that is now my home. I've lived here for a year. It's perfect for people like me.

I find a note lying on my bed.

Hello Gray,

We're still waiting.

Worse. Life is so much worse.

Lauren

"It wasn't your fault, Sean."

"It was an accident."

"A terrible tragedy. She was so young."

"How are you? Are you doing okay?"

"Please don't blame yourself. It wasn't your fault."

It wasn't your fault.

It wasn't your fault.

But it *was* his fault.

His fault for not paying attention. His fault for driving too fast. His fault for asking her to join him that day, for being late to pick her up, for choosing that moment to take his eyes off the road, to look at her, to see the pain in her eyes. He needed to see the pain because he knew it would torment him. As well it should. He was the reason it was there.

But the pain was only there for a moment. One brief, fleeting moment. Then it was gone, eviscerated by the sudden and disorienting impact of the crash.

Then *she* was gone. She'd loved him. And he'd killed her.

Everyone—the doctors, his mom, her sister, their friends—insisted over and over again that it wasn't his fault. They reminded him that it was an accident. They urged him to forgive himself.

"You know that if Beth were still here, she would have already forgiven you."

But he knew the truth. That while these grieving loved ones were assuring him that they didn't blame him, that he had no reason to feel guilty, they were all thinking the same thing: *Thank God it wasn't me*. They wouldn't know how to live with themselves. No one in their right mind would know how to live with themselves. Yet somehow, they expected him to. And maybe if he'd only killed her, he would have eventually learned to adapt. But he'd betrayed her and he'd broken her. And for that, he could never forgive himself.

It had happened the night before the accident. He'd been out drinking with a few of his buddies. They'd planned on making it an early night. He'd just closed out his tab and was in the process of pulling his jacket on when she approached him. He recognized her immediately.

"Lauren," he'd whispered.

"Hey, Sean," she'd smiled at him.

For Sean Behrens, Lauren Crawley was the one that got away. They began dating their sophomore year of college and had only broken up because she had been offered a job out of state. They tried to make the long distance work. More than once, Sean had even considered buying a ring, hopping on an airplane, and proposing to her. He could have done it. Packed up his life in small town Denison, Texas and made the move to big city Chicago. But something always held him back, insisted that he wouldn't belong there, that she had moved on and so should he. And so he did. Fifteen years later, he was happily engaged to Beth Sullivan.

But he never told Lauren that.

He knew he shouldn't have offered to buy her a drink. But he truly believed that he could keep the evening platonic. After all, he loved Beth. She was bright, beautiful, sweet, funny. Beth was the woman he was going to marry. Lauren was a woman he hadn't seen in over a decade. Surely no harm would come from him buying her one drink.

But one drink quickly became two drinks. Two became three. And innocent conversations about their respective lives rapidly evolved into sentimental reminiscences, and Sean found himself regretting his decision to ever let her go. And by the time he finished his last drink of the night, he'd already invited her back to his place for the night.

Drunk as he'd been, Sean remembered every moment of their passionate reunion: how smooth her skin had felt next to his, the soft glow of moonlight reflecting in her pale blue eyes, the faint scent of lilac in her golden hair... And not once, not once had he thought of Beth. It was only as Lauren was kissing him awake the next morning that he realized what he'd done.

"What's the matter?" Lauren had asked him.

"Lauren..." he'd muttered, his own heart aching at the thought of breaking hers. "I have a fiancée."

At first, she looked like she hadn't heard him correctly.

"What?"

"I'm getting married. Her name is Beth. I'm supposed to pick her up this morning. We're... we're going to meet with the florist."

"I don't believe this."

"Lauren, I'm sorry. I—"

"*Don't* talk to me."

And with that, she scooped up her clothes, dressed, and stormed out the door. Sean didn't try to follow her.

He hadn't known how he was supposed to face Beth. She knew him better than anyone. One look was all she'd need to know that something was tormenting him.

Sure enough, she had no sooner climbed into the passenger seat of his car before she asked, "Is everything okay? You look terrible."

"I'm fine," he lied. "I just... didn't sleep very well last night."

But of course, he'd ended up confessing everything to her anyway, mere seconds before the car accident that had claimed her life. In his thirty-seven years, Sean Behrens had come to regret many things, but he would never regret anything so much as his decision to tell Beth the truth in that moment. If he'd waited a second longer, she could have died peacefully, still believing that her fiancé was a good man who would never, ever hurt her. Instead, the last thing she experienced was the sting of betrayal, the shattering of everything she'd come to trust. And his last memory of her would forever be the look of utter devastation on her beautiful face.

It was his fault. Everything was his fault.

The funeral was torture. More than once, Sean had to excuse himself to the restroom to dry heave. He didn't have enough in his system to throw up, but his body was still rebelling against him.

The third time he emerged from the restroom, he saw her. Standing there near the church's entrance, in a simple black dress, her blonde hair tied up in an elegant bun. He blinked, bewildered. It couldn't be her. It didn't make any sense. But it was her.

Lauren.

Curiously, cautiously, he approached her.

"What are you doing here?" he asked.

"I heard about what happened. I wanted to make sure you were okay."

"Are you serious? No, I'm not okay," he snapped. He knew his anger was misdirected, but he couldn't help but feel that she'd crossed a line by showing up at Beth's funeral. He knew she was angry with him, but this was downright inappropriate. "Listen, you can't be here."

"Why not?" she asked, looking perplexed.

"You know damn well why not."

"You weren't so quick to kick me out of your bed the other night. And I certainly shouldn't have been there." Then she reached out and straightened his tie. "Listen. I know this is a troubling time for you. You're feeling guilty and confused. But look on the positive side."

"What are you talking about? There is no positive side."

"Of course there is. Now that Beth is dead, you and I can be together."

Sean was so horrified by her suggestion that he found himself rendered speechless. But before he could come to his senses, his brother, Kevin, called out to him.

"Sean, it's almost over."

"Get out," Sean hissed at Lauren before turning on his heel and walking back to the sanctuary.

"I'll see you soon, baby," she bid him. Sean bit his tongue, determined not to acknowledge her again. Thankfully, Kevin had already disappeared back into the church.

In the days that followed, Sean spent countless hours sitting in the cemetery, atop the fresh mound of brown earth that covered Beth's casket. He spoke to her in a hushed voice, almost as one might murmur a prayer in a quiet cathedral. He apologized profusely, begged her forgiveness, proclaimed his love for her over and over and over again. But nothing he said or did brought him a moment's peace. He was broken.

On the fourth day, as he stood to leave, he noticed the woman watching him from just beyond the trees that lined the perimeter of the graveyard. Lauren had returned.

"Are you following me?" he demanded.

"I'm checking on you," she corrected him. "I'm worried about you."

"It's not your place to worry about me."

"Of course it is. I care about you, Sean."

"If you really care about me, then stay away from me."

"But why?"

"*You have to ask*?" Sean yelled. He'd never seen this side of Lauren before. The Lauren he knew was kind, gentle, understanding. This Lauren was clingy, childish, possibly even a little deranged.

"Please don't push me away, Sean. You shouldn't be alone right now."

"I'm not alone." That was a bold-faced lie. He'd pushed everyone away. He didn't deserve the showering of love and forgiveness that the rest of his friends and family had bestowed upon him. They should have been condemning him.

"Sean, why don't you let me take you home—"

"No."

"I don't think you know what you're saying."

"I know *exactly* what I'm saying. Get out of here, Lauren. I don't want to see you again." When she didn't budge, he yelled, "GO!"

"Oh, darling," she sighed. But finally, she did as he asked. Sean heaved a sigh of relief as he watched her walk away, but the sensation was short-lived. He couldn't shake the feeling that she would be back. And sooner rather than later.

He was right.

She appeared again a few nights later. It was around nine o'clock in the evening and Sean had just settled into his makeshift bed on the couch. He hadn't been able to sleep in his own bed since his night with Lauren. It felt dirty to him now. So he'd been spending his nights on the couch, watching mindless sitcoms on TV until the early hours of the morning. He resisted sleep because when he slept, he dreamt of Beth and woke up with a cold, hollow pain in his gut.

That night, he had just turned off all the lights in his living room when a dark, shadowed figure passed swiftly and soundless by the window. He nearly jumped out of his skin before he caught a second glance and realized it was Lauren, dressed in a white, flowing nightgown and pacing around his backyard, completely barefoot.

Ignore her, he told himself. *Ignore her and she'll go away.*

But when he looked again, she was standing at his back door, staring inside. She'd seen him. And she knew he'd seen her.

"Let me in, Sean."

"No!" he declared, rising up off the couch and storming over to the door. "I don't know what the hell you're thinking, prowling around here like a damn stalker, but if you aren't out of my yard and off my property in thirty seconds, I'm calling the cops."

"Please, just open the door. Let me talk to you."

"Don't you get it, Lauren? I am *done* talking to you. The other night was a mistake. You know it and I know it. Now I just want to forget it."

"You *can't* forget it, Sean. Don't you see that? And it's because we're supposed to be together. This is destiny."

"This is not destiny. This is a nightmare. Now get out of here!"

Lauren simply started at him with those wide, blue eyes.

"You're not going to call the police," she stated.

"The hell I'm not! Why wouldn't I? I've got a crazy person standing on my back porch!"

"If you call the police, they'll want to know the whole story. And the last thing you want is for people knowing that you were in bed with another woman the night before you killed your precious fiancée. This is a small town, after all. Once one person knows, everyone knows."

He didn't want to admit it to her, but she was right. Heaving a reluctant sigh, he unlocked the door and let her in.

"Listen, Lauren. I'm sorry I've been so short with you. I know that what happened between us isn't fair to you. But... you've got to understand that I can't be with you."

"Why not? I know you want me."

"I've already told you, the other night was a mistake. And yes, I admit it. I did want you. You were my first love and I'll always have feelings for you. But we will never be together. I need you to accept that."

But it was as though Lauren hadn't even heard him, as though she'd gone into some sort of trance. Without a word, she closed the space between them and reached up to stroke his face.

"I know you want me," she repeated, her voice barely a whisper.

"Lauren," Sean said, drawing in a shaky breath. "You need to leave."

"I know you want me."

"Stop it."

"You want me."

"*Stop saying that. I* don't *want you! I want Beth!*"

"But Beth is dead. And you killed her," Lauren reminded him gently. "You killed her so that we could be together."

"No! No!" Sean screamed, fighting back tears.

"There, there, baby. Please don't be upset. I love you, too."

"I do *not* love you," Sean hissed. "Get out of here, Lauren. And please, if you care about me at all, please do not come back."

Lauren looked at him with sad, pitiful eyes.

"Very well, Sean. I'll stay away."

He wasn't reassured.

A few days later, Sean ventured into town. It was his first real outing since the accident. He'd wanted to avoid any places that might remind him of his time with Beth, any people who may have known her and who wanted to know how he was doing. But he needed a break from the monotony of grieving inside his own home or at her graveside. Even if it was a brief trip to the local brewery, a few moments in the real world would hopefully do him at least a little bit of good.

It did. When he returned home, he felt, for the first time since the accident, that he was able to see through the haze of depression and guilt that had blanketed his very being since the moment he found out that Beth was gone. He still had a long way to go, but it was enough to give him the slightest sense of hope. And best of all, he hadn't seen nor heard from Lauren. He was so encouraged, in fact, that when Kevin called him and asked if he could take him to dinner the following evening, he gladly accepted.

"So, how are you doing?" Kevin asked once they were seated. "I know, that's probably a stupid question and you're sick to death of hearing it. But you're my brother. I have to ask."

"I'm not okay. I don't know if I'll ever really be okay again. But... I think I'll eventually learn to get by. I guess I'll have to."

"Look, man. I can't even begin to imagine what you're going through right now. I just want you to know that I'm here for you. If you need anything at all, if you need to talk, you know you can call me."

In that moment, Sean almost confessed everything. After all, if he couldn't trust his brother with his innermost demons, who could he trust? And yet, just as he'd opened his mouth to speak, a beautiful girl with long blonde hair walked into the diner and took a seat on the opposite side of the room.

"Oh, you've got to be kidding me," Sean muttered.

"What?" Kevin asked.

"Just..." Sean sighed. "It's nothing."

"Are you sure? You know, if you need to talk to someone, or maybe even go see a psychiatrist, there's no shame."

"I said it's nothing!" Sean snapped, turning half the heads in the diner, including Lauren's. She didn't look at all surprised to see him. In fact, the moment he caught her eye, she sent him a spine-chilling half-smile, like he should have known that she wouldn't stay away for very long.

Fighting every impulse to confront her, Sean remained seated, but he could feel the weight of her gaze smothering him for the remainder of the night. After he and Kevin finally paid their checks, Sean excused himself to the restroom so that he could slip out the back door. He didn't want to pass Lauren. He didn't want to give her the opportunity to reach out to him.

As it turned out, though, she didn't need it. The next day, when he stopped by the local farmer's market, she was there. Later that week, when he stopped by the florist to buy fresh roses for Beth's grave, she was standing just outside the window. He found no refuge at home, because every night, she would sit beneath the magnolia tree in his backyard and run her fingers through the grass while she waited for him to approach her.

Perhaps this was her sick, twisted way of seeking revenge. Maybe she didn't want him at all. She just wanted him to suffer for the pain he'd caused her. It wouldn't make much sense, but it made more sense than accepting that the woman he thought he'd loved so many years ago had completely lost her mind. Whatever her intentions, it was getting harder and harder to ignore her, and sooner or later, others were going to start catching on as well.

Almost as though she had read his thoughts, Lauren stood and walked to the back door.

"How long are we going to do this, Sean?" she called.

Sean didn't respond. Instead, he leaned up against the hallway wall, slid to the floor, and pulled his knees to his chest. He squeezed his eyes shut and covered his ears with his hands.

"Go away. Please just go away," he murmured.

"You don't want that, baby." Her voice startled him. He glared up at her.

"No. No. How did you get in here?" he demanded.

"Your spare key. The one you keep under the brick, remember?"

"How did you know about that?"

"Oh, darling. We're going to spend the rest of our lives together. I should know where you keep your spare key."

"Stop it! *Stop* saying that! We are *never* going to be together because you —"

But then, Sean noticed something that stunned him into silence. He couldn't think. He could barely breathe. He could only stare, light-headed and horrified, at the diamond ring glittering from Lauren's third finger.

Beth's ring.

"Lauren," he murmured, trying to calm his staggering heart. "Where did you get that?"

"What are you talking about, baby?"

"That ring! Where did you get that ring?"

"You don't like it?"

"That is *Beth's engagement ring*!" he screamed, lunging for her hand. But she managed to slip away.

"Not anymore."

"How did you get that?" Sean demanded.

"Why should it matter? She's not using it anymore." Then she sighed. "It really was a lovely viewing, wasn't it? She looked so... peaceful."

Sean's blood ran cold and his heart dropped to the pit of his stomach as he realized what she was telling him.

"You *bitch*," he hissed.

"Now, now, Sean. It's such a beautiful ring. What a shame it would have been for it to be buried six feet down. Besides, I think most people would agree it looks much better on my finger than it ever did on hers."

"You're sick, you know that? You're sick. I'm calling the police," he announced, whipping out his smart phone.

"Are you sure you want to do that?" Lauren wondered. "By the time they get here, I'll have gone. And it will be long enough to tell people the truth: that you wanted Beth dead so that you could be with me. Why else would you give me her ring?"

"*I never gave you that ring*. You stole it! You stole it out of a dead woman's coffin!" Now, Sean was livid. "You've been planning this, haven't you? Since the moment you spotted me in that bar!" Then, something even more terrible dawned on him. "How did you know I would be there that night?"

"Oh, Sean..."

"You knew... Because you've been following me! You knew I was getting married. You knew about Beth. You knew *everything*!" It took every ounce of concentration and control he possessed to keep from dissolving into a full-blown panic attack. "I bet you drugged my drink that night! You did, didn't you?! That's why I took you home! That's why I was stupid enough to... Oh, my *God*..."

"Sean, please, you're being irrational—" Lauren tried to reach out to him, but he slapped her away.

"No! Don't touch me! I'm calling the cops." With trembling fingers, he dialed 911 and held his phone up to his ear.

"911. What's your emergency?"

"Hello. This is Sean Behrens. I'm at 3213 Hillcrest Rd. And I need to report a robbery and a stalker."

"You'll regret this," Lauren sighed. Then she turned and fled.

When Officers Pike and Linley arrived at the scene moments later, Sean described in vivid detail his last encounter with Lauren. He recounted every instance of stalking, every confrontation. Finally, he confessed to their night of passion.

"But I think she drugged me. This woman... She's crazy. The lengths she's gone to... I never thought it could happen to me. How anyone could become that obsessed... She even stole my fiancée's ring. Right out of her casket. You've got to find this woman. You've got to lock her away, or at least get me a restraining order."

"We'll do all we can, Sean. You have our word on that," Officer Andrew Pike assured him. "We just need a few more details for our report. This woman, what did you say her name was?"

"Lauren. Lauren Crawley. She just moved here from Chicago, but to tell you the truth, I don't know how long she's been back."

"Lauren Crawley?" Officer Patricia Linley asked. "That's impossible."

"Why?" Sean asked, his heart pounding with dread. Had Lauren already planted her twisted story? Spread her phony alibi? "Why is it impossible?"

"Sean... My God, I thought you knew."

"What?"

"Lauren died in the accident, Sean. The same one that killed Beth."

"H-How... What? No. That's... That's not right. She - she wasn't there. Beth and I were alone."

"That's true. But that accident occurred because you collided with another car. And Lauren was driving that car. I know this is a lot to take in..."

But her voice had faded to barely an echo in Sean's mind. What she was telling him wasn't real. It wasn't.

It couldn't be...

"Goodbye, Sean."

Instinct

It's sort of an odd time to go camping. The trees are bare, the sky is gray, and the air smells of fresh ice crystals and distant fireplaces. Most are not suited for the great outdoors in early January. But the cold has never affected me the way it might a human. My blood has always run just a little bit hotter.

As for my friends, they don't seem to mind the frigid temperatures either. They're all incredibly eager for a few days at the cabin. Hunter, especially. He keeps talking about hiking and drinking hot cocoa and cuddling beneath a plaid, flannel blanket beside the fireplace. Of course, that last one, he saves just for me. Every time he mentions it, I can't help but blush.

I was not supposed to fall in love with Hunter Isaacs. I wasn't even supposed to befriend him. He's not a member of the pack. He's not even a Wolf. But you know, I think that's why I like him. He's so different from the guys that I grew up with. The guys in the pack.

I was born into a family of Wolves. My father is a natural born Wolf. My mother is a human. Most natural born Wolves are male. In fact, I'm the first female to be born to our pack in at least seven generations. But I'm not like my father or my brother. I don't transform. Or I guess I should say that I can't transform. The made females, the ones who have been bitten or scratched, transform like their mates under the light of the Full Moon, but for reasons that the elders have never been able to understand, natural born females do not.

It used to bother me as a child. I actually envied my older brother, Eamon, and his best friend, Marcus. Once a month, they got to run wild and free as these fierce, magnificent, powerful creatures while I sat at home with my mother. Every once in a while, she would read me a story or braid flowers into my hair, but most of those nights, she would sit by the window, gazing at the Moon, and waiting for my father to return. Even to this day, he holds a strange power over her, like a spell. Or perhaps a curse.

In my younger years, I found their love story to be just that: a love story. Beautiful, inspiring, a real-life fairy tale. I dreamed of marrying a fellow Wolf. But the older I got, the more I began to realize that my mother didn't have much of a life outside of her relationship with my father. She doesn't have any friends. She rarely goes out. Her entire world revolves around my father and the pack. And that notion, which had once seemed so incredibly romantic, began to scare me.

Wolves prey upon partners who need to be needed, need to be controlled, need to be overpowered. Independence and a strong will are considered very unattractive qualities in a potential mate. Of course, as a natural born female I'm expected to marry a member of the pack. Wolves are all about strength and power. If an Alpha can be born to a Wolf and a human woman, imagine the offspring of an Alpha and female Wolf. That baby could very well grow up to be invincible. That's why, ever since we were old enough to understand the concept of marriage and mating, Marcus has had his eye on me. As future Alpha, he will pair with whoever he thinks will bear him the most powerful heirs.

I think it goes without saying that as a sixteen-year-old junior in high school, this isn't the kind of stuff that most girls my age are thinking about. They spend their days giggling over the cutest members of their favorite bands, painting their nails, hanging out at the mall after school... and I wanted that. An escape from the world of Wolves and curses and the ever-demanding Moon.

Then I met Lindy Martinez. We'd had classes together for two years, but we never really spoke until we were paired up for a project in chemistry. I'd never had a human friend before. Not because there are any rules forbidding Wolf and human interaction. It's just that most Wolves and their human mates tend to think they're somehow superior to those who live outside of the circle. And they don't bother making a secret of it.

Long story short, Lindy and I quickly became best friends. She introduced me to the world of normal teenagers: of Friday afternoons at the movies, of football games and pep rallies, of Homecoming dresses, and of girls' nights spent swapping secrets and eating ice cream straight out of the tub. She also introduced me to Hunter.

Of course, I knew of Hunter Isaacs. He was our school's star athlete. He played football in the fall and baseball in the spring. He was also the only guy who'd ever had the nerve to stand up to Eamon Tanner and Marcus King. Over the years, they'd been involved in numerous altercations which usually ended up with at least one of them in the nurse's office and all three of them in detention. To Eamon and Marcus, Hunter was a fool. To Hunter, Eamon and Marcus were bullies.

And yet, Hunter didn't hold the fact that I'm Eamon's younger sister against me. He welcomed me into their group of friends with a warm handshake and a smile that all but took my breath away.

That smile is all I see right now as we pull up to the back door of a rustic yet charming cabin in the woods.

"What do you think, Rae?" he asks me.

Honestly? It's a home after my own heart, even if it isn't technically my home. Still, when I'm with Hunter and Lindy, I feel like I'm home, more so than I've ever felt with the pack.

"I think it's perfect," I tell him.

"Do we really have to go back to school on Monday?" Lindy laments. "Can't we just live here for the rest of our lives?"

"I wish," Tad, Lindy's date for the weekend, remarks. "I'm not ready for another semester of having my butt handed to me on pre-cal's silver platter."

"I've told you I'd be happy to help you study," Lindy reminds him.

"Somehow, I don't think that would be very effective," I tease. It's not that Lindy isn't smart. She is. She'll probably be Valedictorian next year. But when she and Tad are together, they can barely keep their hands off each other. They're actually worse than Hunter and me, which is remarkable considering my animalistic instincts and his amazing biceps.

"Shut up, Rae," Lindy grins.

Once we've unloaded the car and carried all our suitcases inside, it's time for a grocery run. We'd originally considered bringing food, but then Hunter remembered a small, local store where we can shop for the essentials. We determined it would be more sensible and more fun to shop after we arrived.

We step back outside into the frigid, January air and trek through the newly fallen snow to the car. Lindy, in a moment of pure euphoria, runs and jumps onto Tad's back. Caught off guard, he yelps and falls face forward into a snowbank. Hunter and I can't help but laugh.

"Traitor."

It's a hushed, harsh voice, barely a whisper on the wind, but it sobers me up almost immediately. I'm not even sure it's really there. But even if it isn't, the word strikes an icy chord in my heart. To my family, to my pack, I am a traitor.

I was supposed to be with them this weekend. Saturday night marks the first Full Moon of the year. Traditionally, in the days leading up, the packs gather together to feast, to welcome new members, and to celebrate new beginnings. This year's Gathering is to be extra special, as the first Full Moon is also a Blood Moon, one that entices all beings that humans have written off as mythical or legendary: the Wolves, vampires, necromancers, and demons. Every class of monster and nightwalker will be on the prowl come Saturday evening. Except me. I'll be safe, here in my cozy cabin, trying to pretend I don't know who or what may be roaming the very woods just outside my window.

Even though I cannot transform, I can feel the Blood Moon approaching. My senses, already far keener than those of my human friends, are sharpening. I can see farther, hear clearer, and the scent of everything around me is almost overpowering. I'm also faster and stronger than I would be at any other point in the lunar cycle. The Full Moon's power always enhances my abilities, but the Blood Moon sends them into hyper-drive.

"Hey, are you okay?" Hunter asks, wrapping an arm around my shoulders. For a human, he's incredibly perceptive.

"Yeah, I'm fine," I assure him, wondering if those words are ever spoken in complete honesty. "I'm just hungry, that's all."

"Oh God, me too," Tad exclaims. "I haven't eaten all day."

"What about that bag of beef jerky you polished off on the ride up here?" Lindy asks.

"Road trip snacks don't count as food," Tad reasons.

Lindy raises an eyebrow, but she lets him have his moment. Whatever that moment may be.

Like the cabin, the store itself is small and cozy but stocked to the brim with anything and everything we could ever need, from bags of firewood to fleece blankets to cocoa mix and tiny marshmallows.

"Why don't we split up?" Lindy suggests. "Boys, you go and get the firewood, lighter fluid, and whatever you'll need to grill your burgers tonight. Rae and I will get the rest."

"Don't forget the s'mores makings!" Hunter implores us.

"We won't," I promise. As if I need him to remind me. I've never had a s'more before. Most Wolves don't have much of a taste for sweets, and fewer still appreciate the simplicity of roasting marshmallows by a campfire. They'd rather be wrestling or hunting or finding some other way to establish their dominance over one another. As you can imagine, that mentality gets very old very quickly. But I can't wait to roast marshmallows around the fire tonight.

While Lindy and I peruse the back of the store for breakfast essentials - eggs, bacon, butter, and milk - I accidentally tune into a conversation between two men a few aisles over.

"This again?" the first man groans.

"I'm tellin' you, out in these woods, under that Full Moon, you can never be too careful," his companion argues.

"And just what do you think is out there anyway? Frankenstein? Bigfoot? The Loch Ness Monster? Oh no, wait. Don't tell me. Your wolfman!" The first man appropriately howls with laughter.

I freeze in my tracks.

"Yeah, yeah, laugh it up, but I know what I saw. A man, standin' stark naked beneath a tree, transformed into a great gray wolf before my very eyes! I'm tellin' you, they're out there! Whole packs of 'em!"

"If that's so, how come no one else has ever seen one? Why aren't there news crews scanning these woods for your rabid werewolves?"

"There are reports out there if you'd ever bother to look for them! Ever since the eighteen hundreds, packs of wolves have been reported in this area and if you look at the patterns, sightings are three times as likely to be reported the night of a Full Moon!"

This isn't the first time I've overheard a human claim that he's come into contact with one of us, but he's certainly the most adamant. I can't help but wonder, as I glance over my shoulder, if he'd recognize a Wolf in his or her human form.

Turned Wolves keep their same physical characteristics from their lives before, but natural borns all bear a striking resemblance to one another. Our features are sharper that most humans'. According to Lindy, my ears and cheekbones make me look like an elf from Middle Earth. I suppose there are worse mythological creatures to be compared to. Werewolves, for example.

Along with the ears and the cheekbones, our coloring is earthier and more subdued. My brother and I have the same golden amber eyes as most members of our pack, but our hair is a sandy tan color while most of the Wolves we know are a few shades darker. Marcus, with his luscious brown hair and golden eyes, is considered a total heartthrob by most of the girls at our high school. I used to be among them. But now, I think Hunter, with his auburn hair and pale blue eyes, is much cuter.

As though summoned by my thoughts, he sneaks up behind me and grabs me by the waist. For once, I gasp.

"I actually got you!" he exclaims with an endearing sense of triumph.

I've never startled easily, thanks to my Wolfish super senses, but I was so caught up eavesdropping on the man who claimed that he'd seen a werewolf that Hunter actually caught me off guard.

"Enjoy your moment. It won't happen again," I tease as the two men round the corner into my line of vision.

They look exactly how you'd expect a couple of old, weather-beaten, country guys to look. Dressed in jeans, flannel, and hunting jackets, they're both sporting salt-and-pepper beards and John Deer caps. They might even be brothers. Thankfully, they walk right past me without so much as a glance.

"Well, I think we have enough food," Tad remarks, glancing down at both of our incredibly full shopping carts. That's a bit of an understatement. We've accumulated more food than we could ever hope to eat in three days, but at least we won't go hungry if there's a blizzard and we get snowed in.

When we arrive back at the cabin, we immediately set about preparing dinner. Even though Hunter and Tad are anxious to fire up the grill, it's beginning to snow. So instead of hamburgers, we opt for the classic homemade standby, spaghetti and tomato sauce. While Lindy boils the pasta, she instructs the guys on preparing the side salads. In the meantime, I whip up some buttered garlic and basil bread. If nothing else, it will keep the vampires away.

These are the kind of moments I missed out on growing up with the pack. Life's simplicities don't hold a lot of value for creatures who insist on being defined by their strength, position, and power.

"Turning your back on your own kind. And for what? A human halfwit who would have nothing to do with you if he knew the truth."

That's what Marcus said to me the day I officially began dating Hunter. I don't know why it's stayed with me. Hunter and I have been together for about two months now. I'm happier than I've ever been in my life. And yet I can't get those words out of my head. Not because I feel any sort of guilt or shame. If the pack thinks I betrayed them, that's their problem, not mine.

No, the feeling I can't seem to shake is the fear that Marcus is right: that if Hunter knew the truth about me, about what I really am, he wouldn't look at me the same way anymore. He wouldn't see the girl who laughs at all his silly jokes or raced with him through piles of autumn leaves. He would only see the Wolf. The half breed.

The monster.

Part of me finds contentment in knowing that he never has to find out. The other part of me fears that it's only a matter of time until he does.

After dinner, Tad suggests a game night by the fireplace.

"I'm in," Lindy smiles. "But first, I'm changing into my pajamas. Who's with me?"

Although I'm secretly eager to play in the snow, I know that we have a full day of winter hiking to look forward to tomorrow. With that in mind, I follow Lindy into our shared bedroom and dig my pajamas out of my suitcase.

"Oh, my God," she murmurs, glancing down at her phone. "My mother will not stop texting me. First, she wants to make sure I remembered my boots. Then she wants to remind me that this kind of weather can often make roads hazardous and that I need to text her every time we leave the cabin. Now she's asking me if we plan on making a campfire and if so, don't forget to put it out all the way or else the entire cabin might go up in flames."

"Your mother is very cautious," I comment. I've only met Mrs. Martinez twice, and both times, I got the distinct feeling that she knew what I was. Or she at least suspected that I wasn't fully human.

Her overbearing nature aside, I have to admit I envy Lindy's relationship with her mother. Mrs. Martinez loves and cares for Lindy in a way that has never come naturally to my mother. When I announced that I was going to be skipping our annual Gathering for a weekend in the woods with my friends, she didn't beg me to be safe or remind me to pack a warm jacket. She lectured me for my selfishness, my lack of loyalty to my pack, my utter disrespect for the wonderful life I've been given.

"Do you know what it was like for me before I met your father? My life was dull, meaningless. I hesitate to even call it a life. I merely existed. You were lucky enough to be born into this pack. You live every day in a world that others don't even dare to dream exists. You live in a real-life fairy tale. But you're too stubborn and arrogant to appreciate it."

I didn't bother pointing out to my mother that in most fairy tales, the Wolf is rarely the hero.

88

Lindy and I emerge from our bedroom dressed in our warm, flannel pajamas to find the guys have already got a fire going. The smell of the cedar logs is rich and soothing and I find myself closing my eyes as I savor the scent.

"Well done, gentlemen," Lindy says, her voice snapping me out of my trance.

"Wow. Don't you ladies look all cute and cozy," Tad remarks.

Hunter doesn't say anything. He just grins that sweet, friendly, adorable grin as he stands to wrap his arms around me. Firelight dances in his light blue eyes and illuminates the red-gold in his hair. If I listen closely, I can actually hear his heart beating inside his chest. It accelerates as I rise up on my tip toes and press my lips to his cheek. Everything about him is absolutely endearing, and it hurts my heart to think that in a way, he represents the life my mother so callously rejected.

This is my fairy tale. Right here. This snow-covered cabin in the frosty woods, nestled beside a roaring fire, with friends who accept me, and a guy who blushes when I kiss him. Everything is perfect.

Except...

Just now, outside the window, I could swear I saw a shadow, a figure, darting between the trees. It could be anything: a deer, a coyote, an ordinary wolf, maybe even a star-crossed hiker who lost his way. But as I listen, I hear soft and deliberate footsteps just a few meters beyond the cabin's front door. Whoever - or whatever - is out there, is here on purpose.

"Having fun in there, little sister?"

Eamon.

I knew it. I knew, deep down, that the pack would never really let me go. That I could never fully escape. But I never expected him to follow me here.

"We know you can hear us," a second voice taunts. Marcus.

They're not supposed to be here. They're supposed to be at the Gathering. Why? Why would they come all this way, more than two hours by car, just to get inside my head and ruin what is supposed to be the best weekend of my life?

"You know, there's only one thing missing," Lindy states, blissfully unaware of my brother and his companion listening from the shadows of the snow-covered trees. "Hot chocolate."

"You read my mind, Babe," Tad tells her.

"Do you want a cup?" Hunter asks as our friends scamper into the kitchen.

"Yes, please. But first... I think I left my bag with my toothbrush and everything out in the car." I hope he can't tell I'm lying. I've never been very good at outright fibbing.

"Oh. Well, do you want me to go look?"

"No, no. It will only take a minute."

"But it's dark outside. And it's freezing."

"I promise, I'll be fine. I'll be back before you notice I'm gone."

With that, I slip out without grabbing a flashlight or a jacket. I can see perfectly fine in the dark. And as for the cold, I barely notice it. Neither do Eamon or Marcus. They're both dressed in jeans and t-shirts. Looking at them, you'd think it was a balmy seventy degrees outside.

"What are you doing here?" I demand.

"What do you think?" Eamon asks.

"Well, I know that neither of you is concerned for my safety." It sounds harsh, but most humans are no match for Wolves, even those of us who don't transform. Eamon and Marcus have no reason to worry about me. Which can only mean one thing. "You don't honestly think I'm going to *tell* them, do you?"

While there are no official rules forbidding me from revealing my true nature to my human friends, it is strongly discouraged. Ever since the werewolf became common in mythological lore, true Wolves have shared a common understanding and agreement that we keep to ourselves, our mates, and our pack. As far as I know, no one in recent years has dared to break that unwritten protocol.

"Why not? You're weak," Marcus tells me. "So weak you gave in to the first bumbling idiot to pay you half a compliment."

He's baiting me, I know. Unfortunately, I'm short-tempered enough to bite.

"Why on earth would I *want* them to know? You said yourself that they would have nothing to do with me if they found out."

As soon as the words are out of my mouth, a flash of grim and cunning satisfaction flashes across Marcus' face. And I finally understand. They're not here to protect me or to keep tabs on me. They're here to expose me. To sabotage my relationships with my human friends. To drag me back to the Wolves.

"Tell me, Rae, why on earth would you want to be friends with people who would never accept you as you are?" Marcus asks.

"Because they *do* accept me," I retort. They accept Rae Tanner. Not the Wolf, the girl. The girl who enjoys long road trips and has recently developed a profound appreciation for 1990s sitcoms. The girl who dreams of learning to cook, reading more poetry, and attending Prom with the boy she loves. The girl the rest of the pack never bothered to know. Because to them, she didn't matter. Only her blood, her power, and her potential mattered.

"You're lying to yourself. And you know what? You're lying to them, too," Eamon reminds me.

"How do you think they'd react if they knew we were out here?" Marcus wonders.

"You wouldn't," I whisper. "Please. Eamon, Marcus, I beg you. Please, just go. Go back to the Gathering."

"And what? Leave you here with your precious human riffraff? Unlikely."

I've known Marcus long enough to know that when he looks at me, he sees a prize, one that he believes is rightfully his and one that he is all too eager to fight for. Not out of concern or care for me, but to once again establish his strength and status as future Alpha.

"Guys, please, I - "

That's when the door to the cabin opens and Hunter steps out onto the front porch, shining a flashlight into the woods.

"Rae?" he calls.

I panic, certain that he's seen Marcus and Eamon, but as I quickly glance back over my shoulder, I find they've disappeared.

"Are you okay?" he asks, sprinting over to where I'm standing, nowhere near our car. "I was getting worried."

"No, no, I'm fine. I just... I thought I saw something." It's not a total lie.

"Well, come back inside! You must be freezing." He wraps his arms around me and pulls me to his chest. "Did you find your toothbrush?"

"Huh?"

"Your toothbrush. Was it in the car?"

"Oh! Uh, no. I'll look through my bag again. I probably missed it."

"If you still can't find it tomorrow, we can always go into town and buy you a new one," he assures me. He really is very sweet.

"Thank you." I have to fight to keep my voice from breaking. I know my brother and Marcus can hear every word that Hunter and I speak. And it kills me having to keep that a secret from Hunter. I hate that they've put me in this position. And I hate that I have to spend every waking moment from here on out wondering where they are and what exactly they're planning. Because they're not going to let this go. They're not going to let me go.

"Come on," Hunter says to me. "Let's go get some hot chocolate. I made you a cup with extra marshmallows."

Back inside, Lindy and Tad are already snuggling atop a bed of blankets and pillows on the ground next to the fireplace. They've also set aside a stack of board games for us to play while we sip at our hot cocoa.

As the evening progresses, the fire dies down and the snow begins to fall again. It would be a very peaceful evening. If only we were alone.

That's when a harsh, resounding rap on the door startles all of us.

"What the - ?" Hunter wonders.

"Don't answer it!" I hiss. Not that it matters. If Eamon and Marcus wanted to break down the door, they could.

"Who would be wandering around out here at this hour?" Tad wonders.

"Hikers?" Hunter asks.

"Or serial killers," Lindy murmurs.

On cue, our visitors pound on the door again. Lindy shrieks. I try to steady my breathing.

"*Go away,*" I whisper. "*Please go away.*"

"Shh, it's okay," Hunter tries to comfort me. "We're not the only cabin out here. Hopefully whoever it is just has the wrong address."

Three slow knocks this time. They're teasing us, teasing me, trying to get me to break. I hate that they're here, listening, scaring my friends, but I'm selfishly willing to bet that Eamon and Marcus won't go through with their threats to expose me. If they expose me, they expose themselves. They're scaring us, distracting us, but they're not actually going to do anything.

"Should we answer?" Tad asks.

"No," I insist.

"I agree with Rae," Lindy says.

"But what if they need help?" Tad argues. "What if they're sick or injured? What if we wake up and find a frozen corpse buried beneath the snow?"

"Tell you what. We might be able to see the porch from the window. We turn down the lights and try to catch a glimpse through the curtains. If they look harmless, we answer. If not, we call the police," Hunter says.

"But what if they see you?" Lindy asks.

I'm glad she's trying to dissuade them because I don't know what I would say. *Please don't look because chances are, you'll see my brother and Marcus?* Yeah, right. Of course, if they don't want to be seen, chances are, they're already gone. They will have heard every word we're whispering.

"I'll be careful," Hunter promises, peeking through the curtains. "Huh."

"Who is it?" Tad wonders.

"No one. The porch is empty."

"Are you sure?" Lindy asks.

"Positive. There is no one out there."

"Then they're either screwing with us or waiting for us. Either way, no one is opening that door," Lindy says.

I close my eyes and listen to see if I can hear my brother or Marcus laughing or taunting or sprinting through the snow. But the wind is harsh and they're almost certainly keeping quiet in order to frighten me as well.

"Maybe one of us should sleep out here tonight, you know, to keep an eye on things," Tad suggests.

"I don't know. I think I'd feel better if we were all together," Lindy tells him. This whole experience has clearly shaken her and I can't help but feel that that is all my fault. I'm the one who quite literally led the Wolves to our doorstep.

So instead of saying goodnight and retiring to our bedrooms, we make camp in the living room. Lindy and I take the couches, Hunter and Tad settle down on the floor. One by one, my friends drop off to sleep, but I can't stop listening for footsteps in the snow or my brother's jeers through the trees.

I pray to our Mother Moon that he's gone and that he's taken Marcus with him. But a cool tingling in the pit of my stomach tells me that they're still out there. And that they're waiting.

After a night blessedly absent of further incident, we awake to bright streams of sunlight glittering on a blanket of fresh snow. Although I'm still wary of what the day may bring, our moods are all considerably lighter as we prepare for our morning hike.

Outside, the snow has covered up any evidence of Eamon and Marcus's visit last night. While I do consider that a blessing, it also leaves no indication of where they may be. If they are around, they're far enough to be outside my earshot. Though I resolve not to fully let my guard down, I don't want to let thoughts of my brother and Marcus ruin the remainder of my weekend.

Almost as soon as we step beyond the barriers of the forest, Lindy scoops up a snowball and tosses it at Tad. She misses, and the snow explodes in a cloud of shimmering snow against a tree. But Tad still takes it as an act of war. Within seconds, snowballs are flying back and forth between the two. Hunter and I are laughing on the side until a stray snowball hits Hunter in the ear.

"Oh, it's on!" he exclaims as he, too, reaches down and grabs a snowball.

I don't want to be the only one missing out on the fun, so I take a small pile of snow and mold it into a perfect ball. Almost immediately, the snow begins to melt in my hands so I toss it as quickly as I can.

"Ow! Son of a - " Tad yelps, grabbing the back of his shoulder where my snowball made contact with supernatural speed and force. I gasp.

"I am so sorry, Tad!" I say. In my moment of haste, I hadn't taken the time to remind myself I wasn't among my fellow Wolves.

"That was *you*?" Tad asks. "Jeez, Rae. You've got a heck of an arm. Ow."

"Tad, you're wearing like, three layers. She can't have hit you that hard," Hunter remarks.

"Dude, I am not kidding you. I think I'm gonna have a bruise."

"I'm so sorry," I apologize again.

"It's not your fault. Tad's just being dramatic," Hunter assures me.

"You think I'm being dramatic? You stand there and let your girl hurl one at you."

"Babe, stop it. It was just an accident and you're making her feel bad," Lindy says to Tad. "Come on, let's just go explore."

As we set off into the woods, Hunter wraps an arm around my shoulders and asks, "Are you okay?"

"Yeah, I'm fine. I just hope Tad's okay."

"Oh please, he's fine. He takes hits harder than that every afternoon at football practice. You just startled him that's all."

"Okay, good," I smile.

My relief is short-lived, however, as the sound of crunching snow and a snapping twig from the east catches my attention. I'm sure it's nothing. Probably a rabbit or a deer or perhaps fellow hiker. And yet...

I know they're here.

Eamon and Marcus are out there somewhere. And if they're not watching us right now, they have to at least know that we left the cabin. Now that I think about it, I wouldn't put it past them to break in while we're away.

Before I have time to dwell, however, Lindy screams. I look ahead to see two large wolves, white as the virgin snow, crouched down and poised to attack.

These wolves aren't like us. They're ordinary animals. But they've been influenced by the supernatural. Our elders have never been able to figure out the connection between the common wolf and our pack. There are theories, of course. One is that we're not, in fact, humans cursed by the Moon to transform into wolves, but rather we are wolves who walk around in human skin and that only the Full Moon reveals our true nature.

The why, the how, the history... none of that is important now. All that matters is that these wolves are here for a reason.

"Stay behind me!" Hunter tells me.

But I don't listen. Instead, I take a few tentative steps forward and look the larger wolf in the eye. We don't communicate with words, but I can see - or perhaps, more accurately, sense - what Eamon and Marcus have communicated to him.

Threat.

Danger.

Protect.

Attack.

Kill.

"No!" I exclaim aloud.

The wolves snarl and snap at me in response. The larger one steps forward.

"Rae! What are you *doing*?" Lindy hisses.

"*Come on, come on... Listen to me...*" I whisper, desperately hoping that I can communicate to these creatures that they've been misled by the two Wolves they met earlier.

We pose no threat, no danger.

We're going to leave peacefully.

Please don't attack. Please let us live.

But they've already decided.

"Run," I tell my friends. They remain frozen in their tracks. "*Run!*"

And so we run. And the wolves pursue, growling and snapping at our heals. We duck and dodge trees and low limbs. Out of the corner of my eye, I see Lindy's burgundy scarf dancing around her dark hair as she runs. A dead, crooked tree branch snags the scarf, pulling Lindy backwards into a snowbank as the wolves close in.

"Lindy!" I cry out.

Please, please, not her...

The wolves must sense my plea because they don't attack her. They simply stand over her, growling and drooling and barring their teeth. Lindy whimpers and tries to crawl away, but her scarf is still stuck in the tree.

Before I can stop him, Tad rushes to Lindy's side to try and free her. The wolves, unfortunately, are not inclined to show him the same mercy.

What happens next is a blur. As the wolves prepare to pounce, I leap in front of them in the hopes of shielding my friends.

"Rae, *no!*" Hunter yells at me, but it's too late. The smaller wolf's sharp claws catch the sleeve of my jacket, ripping it and tearing into my flesh. I fight back a scream. I don't want my friends to know I've been hurt, but I'm afraid the blood stains on the snow will betray me as Hunter sprints to my side.

The wolves have figured out by now that I'm one of them, more or less, and they momentarily halt their attack. Thankfully, the momentary distraction has given Tad enough time to untangle Lindy from her scarf.

"Rae! Are you crazy? *Come on!*" Tad yells at me.

We take off running once again and we don't look back until we've reached the cabin.

"Rae, you were scratched by a wild wolf. You need to go to the emergency room," Hunter says.

"For the last time, I'm telling you, I'm fine. It's *barely* a scratch."

Well, now it is. If Hunter had caught a glimpse of the wound before, he would have called 911, no questions asked. But Wolves are fast healers. Now, what once were four gaping crevices in my skin are mere scrapes. They'll probably be gone by morning.

"That's not the point. That wolf could be carrying diseases. If nothing else, you need to be treated for trauma."

"Hunter, I'm not traumatized. I'm not even bleeding. If it would make you feel better, I promise to go to the doctor as soon as we get home. But I don't want to go to the hospital."

"Right now, I don't care what you want. I care about what happens to you."

"Hunter's right, Rae," Lindy agrees. "I know you think you're okay, and you probably are, but it's better to be safe than sorry."

I understand their concern for me, and I appreciate it. But I'm not going to any hospital. I can't. If I go to a hospital, they're going to want to run a bunch of tests and at least one of those tests is likely to include blood work. The minute the doctors get a good look at my blood, they're going to know I'm not human. Well, not completely human. If I ever do need to seek professional healthcare, which is rare, I visit Dr. Mosier, who belongs to a neighboring pack.

"Look, I don't want to go back out there tonight. If I start feeling sick or running a fever or anything of the sort, I will go to the hospital. I'll even let you airlift me in. But for now, all I want is to light another fire, eat a good meal, and try to enjoy this evening," I tell them.

Reluctantly, they agree and although I can tell that they're still worried, slowly, surely, we all begin to relax.

Instead of playing a game as dusk begins to fall, we settle around the television for a movie night. Hunter wraps a heavy comforter around my shoulders before snuggling in next to me. I expect him to immediately turn his attention to the TV, but instead, his gaze lingers on me. I'm not too proud to admit that I'm equally enchanted by him. He's so beautiful, so kind, so protective. Even in the dim light, his blue eyes sparkle as he smiles at me. Like a moth drawn to a flame, or perhaps more accurately, a Wolf drawn to the Moon, I lean in and kiss him silently on the lips.

"Thank you for taking such good care of me," I whisper.

"I feel like I should have done more," he confesses.

"No," I assure him. "You're wonderful." And to prove it, I kiss him again.

Once the movie begins, I rest my head on Hunter's chest and try to absorb the story, but I can't stop my mind from drifting or my eyelids from slipping shut. In spite of a rather trying day, it's easy to find comfort and peace in Hunter's warm embrace.

The next thing I know, I'm being stirred from sleep by a distant howl, too far for my friends to hear. Terrified that it might be Eamon and Marcus, a cold knot begins to form in my stomach. Then I remember that it's only Friday. The Moon won't be full until tomorrow. It can't be them.

That's when I glance out the window. Two large, white shadows slink silently through the trees, right up the steps to our front porch. I can hear their claws *scritch-scratching* as they pace the wooden planks outside the door. My friends hear it too.

"What is that?" Lindy whispers.

"I don't know," Tad says. "Sounds like a raccoon or something."

The wolves paw at the door with so much force that it begins to rattle on its hinges. Lindy gasps and clings to Tad.

"That's not a raccoon," Hunter says. "I think our friends are back."

"What?" Lindy hisses. "No! That's impossible."

But Hunter's suspicions are confirmed when three more wolves appear through the windows around the back porch.

"Want us to call them off, Rae? Our little Rae of Moonlight?" It's a rather cruel taunt, calling me by my childhood nickname. But then, kindness and compassion have never been Eamon's strongest suits.

"*It's simple. Come back with us. Come back to the Gathering,*" Marcus instructs. "*There's still time for you to make things right.*"

I don't acknowledge them. Instead, I hold tightly to Hunter as the wolves at the front door try once more to claw their way in.

"*Maybe we were wrong about her, Marcus. Maybe she doesn't care for those humans as much as we thought she did,*" my brother comments.

"*And why do you say that?*"

"*If she did... You'd think she'd feel at least a little guilty endangering their lives like this.*"

I close my eyes and try to tune out the sound of my heart drumming with a heavy sense of dread. Is that really what I'm doing? Am I really so stubborn, so selfish, that I would put my friends' lives at risk? And for what? A few days in a cabin?

Are you kidding? A small, defiant voice in the back of my mind argues. *You are not endangering their lives. They are. Eamon and Marcus. They are to blame. Not you.*

"Should we call someone?" Tad wonders.

"Who would we call? The local animal control?" Lindy asks.

"I'm not sure if there's much they could do..." Hunter remarks.

"Has this ever happened to you before out here?" Tad asks him.

"No, never. I've never seen wolves behave like this."

And for some reason, his statement gives me an idea.

I need to call my dad.

"I'll be right back," I announce.

"Where are you going?" Lindy whimpers.

"I think I know who to call."

I grab my phone and disappear into the bedroom that Lindy and I were supposed to share this weekend. I know my dad was disappointed that I chose to skip out on the Gathering, but he was also the most sympathetic when I told him that I wanted friends, to be accepted. Maybe it's because I'm his little girl. Or maybe it's because he knows what it's like to fall in love with a human. Either way, I hope he can convince Eamon and Marcus to come home and leave us in peace.

"Rae? What is it? Are you all right?" he answers without a hello. My dad isn't exactly what you'd call a phone person. Wolves are surprisingly anti-technology. I guess they think that deep and dark creatures of the night shouldn't have to rely on human gadgets or something. It's a little irritating.

"Yeah, Dad, I'm fine. But I was hoping you could help me with something." Well aware that I sound like a spoiled toddler tattling on her older brother, I tell my father everything.

"And what do want me to do?" my father asks.

"Tell them to stop! Dad, they're out here harassing us! Tormenting my friends, siccing wild wolves on us... Come on, we've never considered humans the enemy. This behavior is just... well, it's wrong!"

"Very well. I will summon Eamon home. He and Marcus should be home for the Blood Moon tomorrow night, anyway."

As should you.

The words are unspoken, but I hear them nevertheless.

"Thank you, Dad."

"Rae," my father speaks my name in a tone that suggests I'm not going to like what he has to say. "I know you think you've found acceptance amongst these humans, but promise me you won't forget who your true allies are, who you truly are. No matter how much you like them, you know you will never really belong with them."

"Oh. Um... Okay..." I murmur, hoping he can't hear the quiver in my voice. I hate crying, and I especially hate crying in front of Wolves. It's considered a weakness, a vulnerability. An admission of defeat. And Wolves never admit defeat.

"I don't mean to upset you. I just don't want you getting too attached. You belong with your own kind, Rae. And I... I don't want to see you get hurt." I know how difficult it is for him to admit this. Displays of affection, even words of affirmation, are not his forte. But I guess it's nice of him to try.

"I know, Dad. Thanks."

It takes another hour before the wolves finally begin to retreat, but once they're gone, a new sense of peace and relief settles over the cabin. Although Tad and Hunter agree to keep watch for any strange activity outside, eventually, we settle back in for our movie night. And this time, as I wrap my arms once again around Hunter's strong torso, I can't help but smile.

It's over. It's finally over.

Saturday, our final full day at the cabin, is perfect. Tomorrow, we'll be packing up and driving back home, but tonight, I can only bask in my own sense of unadulterated bliss. I don't think I've ever had more fun than I've ever had today. Although we didn't wander too far from the cabin, we enjoyed almost a full day outside, sledding and building forts and taking selfies in the snow. I don't want to think about leaving tomorrow. I'm not ready to return to my normal life.

Thankfully, as Hunter reminds me, we'll still have each other. And we have everything to look forward to. Including Prom.

But for now, as the sun begins to set, Hunter and Tad are hard at work preparing the outdoor grill for our final dinner here in the woods while Lindy and I gather wood for the campfire.

"Do you know how to build a fire?" Lindy asks.

"Yeah. My dad taught my brother and me when we were kids." Outdoor survival skills are essential for Wolf pups.

"You don't talk about your family all that much."

"Yeah, well, there's a reason for that." I sigh, lifting several logs that would probably too heavy for an average girl my size into my arms.

"I'm sorry, Rae. We don't have to talk about it. I'm just glad you're here now. I'm glad we're friends."

"I am, too," I smile.

It's only then that I sense we're no longer alone. Terrified that Eamon and Marcus may have returned, I turn swiftly towards the woods. In the distance, I see a man, dressed in a heavy, brown coat and boots. Immediately, I recognize him as the man from the local convenience store.

The one who claims to have seen a werewolf.

But what is he doing all the way out here?

"Evenin', girls," he greets us. Lindy recoils nervously as he approaches us. "I don't mean to scare you or anything. I was patrolling the area and caught a whiff of whatever y'all are cookin' out here. Smells mighty tasty."

"Th-thank you," Lindy answers.

"Don't worry, I ain't askin' to stay or nothin'. I just wanted to stop by and warn y'all not to stay out after dark," he says.

"After dark? Why?" Lindy wonders. Clearly, she didn't overhear his conversation about the supposed wolfman.

"Because tonight's the Full Moon, young lady. And you don't want to be out here in these woods when that Moon begins to shine."

"Um..." Lindy glances at me, unsure of what to say.

"Thank you, sir. We'll keep that in mind," I promise him. But something in my voice must give me away, because his eyes linger on me for a fraction of a second longer than they should.

"You know, don't you?" he asks.

"I'm sorry?"

"You know what's out there. You've seen them too, haven't you?"

"I don't know what you - "

"The wolves!"

"Wolves?" Lindy squeaks.

The man turns his attention back on her.

"That's right, girlie. The wolves. The werewolves."

"Yes! I mean, no! I mean, we were followed by a pack of wolves last night. Came right up to our front door," Lindy tells him.

And immediately, as though he suspects something, his gaze flashes back to me.

"But they - they weren't - werewolves," I stammer. I hate using that word. Werewolf. It's considered a derogatory term in our pack. "They were just wolves. Just ordinary wolves."

"There ain't nothin' ordinary about these woods. Not when the Full Moon is on the rise," the man growls. "Anyway, I best be lettin' you girls get back to your dinner. Sorry if I scared you. Just please... be aware."

"We will, sir," we promise.

As soon as he walks away, Lindy mutters, "That was so weird."

"Yeah," is all I can say.

"You don't think he's right, do you?"

"What?" I ask, trying my best to sound incredulous. "No. Of course not. Nothing but fairy tales and superstitions."

And I hope she believes me. Because I'm not so sure I would if I were her.

After a delectable dinner of burgers and grilled potatoes, we are all full and content. Lindy's jitters have subsided and we all agree that it's finally time to make s'mores.

"Are you ready for this?" Hunter asks me with an adorably cheeky grin as Lindy and Tad retreat back to the cabin to retrieve the graham crackers, chocolate, and marshmallows.

"I was born ready."

"Now *that* is a bold-faced lie."

The new voice sends a sickening chill right through to my very core. Startled, Hunter turns to see Eamon and Marcus emerging from the shadows of the forest, dressed in nothing but old, tattered jeans.

"Then again," Eamon continues, "the truth doesn't exactly come easy to you, does it, Rae?"

"What are you doing here?" Hunter demands, leaping to his feet.

"Why don't you ask your girlfriend?" Marcus says.

"No. No, I'm talking to you," Hunter snaps, storming over to them.

"Hunter, *no!*" I scream and rush after him. It's getting dark outside. Too dark. And the Full Moon is fast approaching. "Stay away. You've got to stay away from them!"

"You gonna tell him why, little sister?" Eamon asks. "Go ahead. We've got all night."

"In a manner of speaking," Marcus sneers.

"They're crazy, Hunter. Get back to the cabin. Now!" I plead.

"Oh yes, we're the ones who sound crazy," Eamon says. "That was really cute of you, you know? Calling Dad, telling him that we were being mean to you and your pathetic little human friends. Did you really think he was going to stop us?"

"*What* are you talking about?" Hunter demands.

Marcus smirks.

"You're about to find out."

As soon as the words are out of his mouth, white Moonlight begins to spill through the trees, illuminating the ice, the snow, and the horrified look on Hunter's face as the bones in Eamon and Marcus's bodies begin to break. They throw their necks back before falling forward, crouching onto their hands and knees. All the while, they grimace and moan, all but howling in the unforgiving light of the Moon.

"Run, Hunter. *Run!*" I beg him.

But it's too late. Their transformation is complete. There is no way to escape them. Hunter's only hope is for the Wolves to show him mercy.

Hunter, stunned by what he's just witnessed, remains frozen where he stands.

"This isn't... This can't be happening..." he murmurs.

"*Run!*" I scream.

Finally, he hears me. He takes off in a mad dash back toward the cabin.

Marcus gives me one last, icy glance. I swear I can see a sick, twisted smile in his Wolfish face, reminding me that while his body may be that of a wild animal, his mind is still as monstrously human as they come.

What happens next is a blur. I see Hunter, running with all his might, through a nightmare that he should never have had to face in the waking world. I see my brother and Marcus, their tails swishing in the Moonlight, as they leap into action. I don't have time to think about whether they mean to scare or kill. Acting purely on instinct, I dart after them. But even at my strongest, I'm nowhere near as fast or powerful as Eamon and Marcus.

That's when I see the man. The stranger from earlier. Instantly, a wave of gratitude and relief washes over me.

He's safe. Hunter's safe.

But then I see the gun, its sleek silver body reflecting the bright, eerie glow of the Blood Moon.

"*NO!*"

He doesn't hear me. None of them do.

The man pulls the trigger and the world around me explodes in a blinding flash of white light and a deafening *BANG!*

Terrified, I crumple to the ground, shielding my ears and squeezing my eyes shut in a desperate attempt to block everything out... and a cowardly attempt to protect myself. Even after the chaos dies down and a haunting stillness settles over the scene, I don't look up.

Only the howl of a lone Wolf, one so mournful that it pierces my heart, compels me to open my eyes. I immediately wish I hadn't.

The man with the gun is dead. Lying next to him, in a pool of fresh blood, is Eamon. He's not moving. He's not breathing. Marcus stands over him, nudging him with his muzzle, beseeching his fallen pack mate to show any signs of life.

No... No... Not Eamon. Please, no...

As the tears for my brother begin to fall, another figure catches my eye. Hunter is kneeling in the snow, grimacing in pain, but blessedly alive.

"Hunter!" I rush to his side.

"Rae..." he moans, grasping at his arm. The sickly, metallic scent of blood fills my nose and turns my stomach as I realize the wound he's trying to cover up is a bite mark.

Bitten. Hunter has been bitten.

And my brother is dead.

And it's all my fault.

"Hunter... I'm sorry... I'm so sorry."

The Kisharliet

They are said to be tall. Tall, merciless, and fearsome. Robed in strange suits of black armor. Weapons always at the ready. Known to the farthest reaches of the farthest galaxy as harbingers of death and destruction.

They are the War-Seekers. The Peace-Stealers.

The Kisharli.

The Zulirum officers always claim that it is only a matter of time, that a Kisharli invasion is imminent. Still, Tibira never imagined she would live to see one with her own eyes. And certainly not in the dusty yard of a Zulirum prison.

"Do not stare, sister," Tirida cautions her. "You do not know of what it is capable."

Tibira knows her sister speaks the truth. All her life, she has heard dreadful tales of the beings that savaged their own planet, their own communities, their own kind. They worship fire and power and hold no love for races or creatures that they deem inferior. The Kisharli are dangerous.

And yet Tibira cannot bring herself to look away.

The Kisharliet that now cowers in fear at the edge of the prison yard is neither large nor threatening. It is smaller, softer, with hair of galactic black, skin that glows a golden brown, and eyes as green as the lush foliage on Tibira's home planet of Veirene. Tears glisten in those eyes now.

How very strange.

"It is afraid," Tibira whispers to Tirida.

"It is an act," her sister warns her. "Do not be deceived."

"Why is it here, I wonder?" Kisharli are rarely seen and almost never captured.

"Is being a Kisharliet not reason enough?" Tirida spits as a lone siren wails thrice, indicating the end of their precious hour outside the prison walls.

"Fall in!" An officer orders.

Tibira and Tirida obey. The Kisharliet resists. Guards are dispatched. And in spite of her sister's warning, Tibira looks back just in time to see those guards seizing the Kisharliet by its hair and frail arms as the pitiful being screams in agony, fear, and fury.

The dream is the same. It is always the same.

Tibira is back home on Veirene. It is a perfect day. Both suns shine in the pale-yellow sky as the Tigiburu birds sing from their nests in her garden. Tibira breathes in the sweet perfume of her beloved flowers as she sets about preparing her studio for the day. A sculptor by trade, she feels a particular passion for her newest project: a carving of the four planets that formed the Sovereign Alliance - peaceful Veirene, loyal Sadura, wise Dihitur, and their reigning world, the mighty Zulir - all floating within a single star to honor those brave soldiers serving in the Royal Zulirum Military.

Soldiers like Tirida.

Then, as though beckoned by her very imaginings, Tirida is there, standing on Tibira's doorstep in the darkest depths of night. At first glimpse, Tibira almost fails to recognize her own sister. Her lavender skin is paler than usual and she keeps her antennae concealed beneath a cloak of black starlight.

"Sister, what are - "

"Shh!" Tirida hisses, ducking inside and quickly shutting the door behind her. Then, taking a deep breath, she closes her violet eyes and crumples to the ground, weeping with tortured relief.

The dream then changes again. It is midday and the Zulirum soldiers have come. They gather at the threshold with great force and with great anger.

"Tibira Vel! By the power of the Sovereign Alliance and the Royal Zulirum Military, I command you open this door and surrender the runaway!"

"Tibira, please... I'm sorry. I'm so sorry... Please, forgive me," Tirida pleads.

"You are my sister. There is nothing to forgive."

Those words now echo in the eerie glow of her prison cell as Tibira stirs to the waking world. Those words that follow her, that haunt her, yet that she cannot bring herself to regret.

Those words are the very last Tibira Vel of Veirene spoke as a free being.

"I overheard the guards talking. They say that it is a monster, that it devoured its own young and bathed itself in their blood."

"I hear it stowed away on a Saduran cargo ship and attempted to slaughter the entire crew. The first mate scarcely escaped with his life."

"Well, I am told that it is betrothed to a high-ranking Kisharli officer but that that officer would rather see it die here than post bond to the Zulirum."

Tibira sits in silence and absorbs the words of her fellow inmates and laborers. The workday has only just begun inside the prison's manufacturing plant and yet, the atmosphere inside the ordinarily dreary factory all but hums with energy and electricity.

"Look! It's here," Nigak, the Deceiver of Dihitur, whispers with urgency.

Every eye turns to see the Kisharliet, looking sad and sickly, gazing down at the tools provided with discernible uncertainty. Although it is dressed in the same oversized white uniform as the rest of them, there is no blending in for the lone Kisharliet. Its mere presence is a blazing spark in an endless, empty sky. It cannot be ignored. It cannot be trusted. It cannot be tolerated.

Or so say the others.

"We must consult with Ubair." Tirida's voice trembles.

"For what purpose?" Tibira wonders.

"We still have rights, even in this wretched place. If we are feeling threatened or unsafe in our own work environment, we have the right to make those feelings known. Ubair is the head of our union. He will have a course of action for us."

"But if the Kisharliet is here, if it is working in our factory, does it not have rights as well?"

"Rights?" Gabguz of Sadura barks in his deep, gravelly voice. "That creature is lucky to still have breath in its vile body."

"Which you would gladly take from it," Tibira accuses. It is no secret inside the prison walls that Gabguz is himself a murderer.

"Don't act like you wouldn't thank me," Gabguz growls back at her.

"Enough," Zirru, the Zulirum Priestess, scolds them. "Waste not your time quarreling when there is work to be done. No good will it do you. Nor anyone."

"Oh, spare us your verses," Gabguz grumbles.

Eccentric though she may be, Tibira finds herself of the same mind as Zirru. Fighting amongst themselves would bring no solace nor solution. Convicts though they all may be, they share a common sense of respect and camaraderie. And nothing, not even the arrival of a Kisharliet, can sever the shackles that bond them.

Instead of working for wages, the inmates of Zulir's prison work to buy their own freedom. The price of that freedom depends on the severity of the crime committed. Tibira is among those who may easily earn their freedom within a few short years. Harboring a fugitive, while a serious infraction of the law, is not, in her instance, considered a dangerous act given that the fugitive in question happened to be her sister. Tirida's crime of abandoning her post and deserting her fellow soldiers, on the other hand, is treason and demands a longer sentence. Nigak sealed a similar fate for himself when he tricked Dihitur government officials into revealing the access code to the planetary treasury.

Then there's Zirru. For months, the imprisonment of the Priestess and her closest followers called into question the power and authority that the Zulirum claim to be their Divine right, for those were the claims that Zirru herself made in the days leading up to her arrest.

"The Zulirum are no more powerful than our neighbors on Dihitur or Sadura or sweet Veirene. Pride and arrogance will be our downfall. Revolution, I have seen."

A small throng of Sadurans attempted an uprising against the Zulirum the morning after her incarceration. They were quickly neutralized, effectively silencing any whisperings of change or rebellion. Years, now, have passed with no further incident. Zirru serves her harsh sentence with no sign of resentment but with no sign of remorse, either. And the Zulirum still reign supreme over all planets and peoples.

Except the Kisharli. That war still rages on. There is no escape from it. Not even behind bars.

Tibira has only an elementary understanding of the war and its history. It began with exploration and necessity. The Kisharli ventured beyond the reaches of their own solar system in the hopes of seeking out a new planet to call home after their reign of ruin and neglect reduced the paradise that once was Kishar to a toxic wasteland. Representatives of the Royal Zulirum Military were prepared to extend an offering of peace and warm wishes to the alien visitors, but upon first contact, the Kisharli opened fire, and any hopes for a harmonious coexistence were obliterated.

This is the case that the laborers present to Ubair at the gathering of their union.

"We cannot work with it."

"Keep it locked away in its cell."

"Why should it be given a chance to work its way back to our enemies?"

"It should be destroyed!"

"Please, calm yourselves!" Ubair, a Zulirum of modest height and great width, raises all four of his hands to silence his comrades in crime. "I understand your concerns, and I agree, the issue of the Kisharliet cannot be ignored. But we also must accept that its presence here may be of great value to us."

This is not what the prisoners want to hear.

"It is of no value! It is worthless!"

"An abomination!"

"It cannot even speak our language!"

"Listen to me! Listen!" Ubair pleads with the heckling crowd. "It is true, the Kisharliet is not versed in our common tongue. But scholars of Dihitur have been studying *their* language in preparation for a day like this one. A day in which we have a vulnerable, weak Kisharliet at our disposal. Now, two Dihitur translators are scheduled to arrive within the hour. If they are, in fact, able to establish communication, it could benefit our fleet tremendously."

"And what if it doesn't want to talk?" Tirida demands.

"Then we *make* it talk!" Gabguz shouts.

"How?" Tibira finally speaks up.

"I'm sure the warden has his ways," Gabguz dribbles, a sadistic grin on his warty face.

"You mean torture?" Tibira is horrified. "No! No, absolutely not!"

But her declaration is met with resistance.

"What concern is it to you?"

"It's just a Kisharliet!"

"If they want to torture it, *let* them torture it!"

"But it is not who we are!" Tibira tries to reason with them, but she is alone in her protest. Torture is a Kisharli weapon, one that the Sovereign Alliance has never condoned. The very idea is enough to leave Tibira feeling faint.

Once again, Ubair raises his hands up in an attempt to silence the crowd.

"The Kisharliet is young and it is fragile. Even if we were to resort to more... extreme methods... it would require very little to break it."

His words offer Tibira no reassurance, but she knows that there will be no arguing with him. So she sits in silence and waits for whatever is to come.

The Kisharliet is compliant. Surprisingly so. Every day, it welcomes the Dihitur translators. Every day, they learn something new. And every day, Ubair reports back to the union.

The Kisharliet fled its home planet with its mate and young ones after their leader declared a state of desolation. They boarded a ship of would-be settlers, seekers of sanctuary, Kisharli refugees. But that ship was attacked. Ransacked. Destroyed. And every being aboard fell victim to a blaze of nuclear fire.

Every being, save for their Kisharliet.

It claims it is scared. It claims it is lonely. It claims it wishes it had never left its home on Kishar. But it does not call its planet Kishar. It does not even know of such a word. It instead calls it by its Kisharli name: Earth.

"Earth," Tibira whispers to herself. It is late afternoon in the manufacturing plant and the sad history of the Kisharliet still haunts her.

"Lies. All lies. It is trying to save its own filthy skin," Tirida hisses under her breath. Tibira makes no response. She simply averts her gaze. Tirida takes notice. "Sister? What troubles you?"

"It is nothing," Tibira answers.

"You are withholding."

"I am tired."

"She pities it," Nigak interjects, his black, beady eyes looking Tibira up and down.

"It? Surely not," Tirida scoffs, drawing the attention of Zirru and her devout followers.

"And if I do?" Tibira speaks softly.

"Tibira." Her sister's face falls and her voice trembles with the utmost gravity. "I know you are of a gentle heart and an artist's curious spirit, but you cannot mean what you say. It is vulgar. It is evil. Nothing good comes from the Kisharli. And nothing good will come of your sympathy."

"But if its story is true - "

"Its story is of no matter. It is a Kisharliet!"

"Yes, and Gabguz is a murderer and yet we still welcome him with respect and acceptance. We still offer him a place in the union. We still call him *friend*."

"Gabguz is one of us! And it would do you well to beseech the deities that be that he hears no tell of this conversation. Lest you hope to be his next victim!"

Tibira is stricken. She has never exchanged such words with Tirida, nor has she ever known her sister to be so harsh. So unjust. So cruel.

It is more than Tibira is able to withstand.

Then Zirru approaches and kneels down before her.

"To share in the grief of another is no weakness, child," the Priestess speaks gently so that only she may hear. "Your strength is in your compassion. For the lowly. For the exiled."

Tibira raises her eyes to meet the Zirru's sparkling amber eyes. The Priestess' smile is warm, her presence comforting. It is then that Tibira knows what she must do. What she wants to do. For the lowly. For the exiled.

For the Kisharliet.

Without a glance back at her sister or Nigak, Tibira rises up out of her seat and, well aware of every gaze, crosses the room to where the Kisharliet sits, alone and frightened. Slowly, Tibira takes the seat directly across from it. And, summoning every ounce of courage that she possesses, she smiles.

"Hello. I'm Tibira," she introduces herself. The Kisharliet stares at her with wide, sunken eyes. It does not understand. Tibira raises her hand and presses it to her beating heart. "Tibira."

Time slows, stops. All is silent. All is still.

Then, a miracle.

A fleeting moment of comprehension.

An overpowering sense of peace.

The Kisharliet smiles back at her.

Then slowly, it lifts its hand and rests it over its own heart.

"Diana."

Crossover
A Boy Band/Cemetery Tours Story

Ode to Pumpkin Spice
A Poem by Melissa Kearney Parker

White twinkle lights illuminate,
The quaint New England town,
As black cats keep their watch by night,
And autumn leaves drift down.

All Hallow's Eve is fast approaching,
And it all seems oh, so nice,
Ghost stories whispered in the dark,
And the smell of pumpkin spice.

But here, you'll find no candied treats,
Just tricks and hints of musk,
There's no such dream as pumpkin spice
Living on a tour bus.

It's well past midnight and everyone is still wide awake.

I thought for sure that by the time I took a shower and changed into my PJs, the guys would have at least settled down a little. After all, they just performed a full-length concert in front of a sold-out crowd for the second night in a row. Then again, knowing them, that's why they're all still wide awake. They're all still on that post-concert high.

"Tonight. Was. The. Best. Night. Of. My. Life!" Jesse declares, live streaming a quick video for all of his adoring fans. "I love you all. Seriously. If I could kiss each and every one of you... I would."

"I don't think the world is quite ready for that," Oliver quips.

"You wanna bet?" Josh laughs from the tiny kitchen. He's standing in front of the microwave, wearing nothing but basketball shorts, and waiting for his popcorn to finish popping.

Cory, meanwhile, is busy browsing YouTube for videos of their performance while Sam is sitting at the breakfast nook and is... drawing a face on a pumpkin? Where did he get a pumpkin?

"What are you doing?" I ask, taking a seat across from him.

"Carving a jack-o-lantern," he answers. "It's the day before Halloween! We have to have a jack-o-lantern!"

"You're not thinking of wielding a knife while the bus is speeding down the highway at seventy miles an hour, are you, Samuel?" Cory asks.

"... No." Which means he absolutely was.

"You know what we *should* do?" Josh asks. "We should take this popcorn, break out the Halloween candy, and watch a scary movie."

"Pass," Jesse declares.

"What's the matter, Jess? Afraid the boogeyman will sneak out to snack on your toes while you're asleep?" Josh teases.

"No," Jesse huffs.

"What is it then? Is it the knife-wielding psycho in the shower? Or the havoc-wreaking poltergeist?" Josh asks. "Wait,

119

it isn't the blood, is it? Because I'll admit, that makes me a little squeamish too - "

"I just don't like horror movies, okay? I think they're... boring..." Jesse feebly defends himself.

"Oh, please. You're such a coward," Joni remarks from her bunk in the next room.

Jesse grimaces and suddenly, teasing him isn't fun anymore. You see, Joni used to be Jesse's girlfriend, but they broke up over the summer. Jesse claims it was a mutual decision. He says that with The Kind of September's first album skyrocketing to the top of the charts and with all the interviews and touring, he and Joni both agreed they were better off as friends and colleagues than boyfriend and girlfriend. According to Joni, the breakup was far less mutual. She'll tell anyone who will listen that Jesse's a jerk who didn't want to be tied down to one person when girls all over the world began throwing themselves at him.

All in all, it's made for a rather awkward two months aboard The Kind of September's tour bus.

By the way, in case you hadn't heard, The Kind of September is the hottest boy band on the planet right now. They began recording singles after we all graduated from high school last year, but it wasn't until they released their first full-length album about six months ago that they became a worldwide phenomenon. Now fans around the world can't get enough of Josh Cahill, Cory Foreman, Oliver Berkley, Jesse Scott, or Sam Morneau. But you know, thankfully, aside from Jesse breaking up with Joni, they really haven't let it all go to their heads. They're still the same goofy guys they always have been.

Now they're just goofy guys with a lot of money and millions of adoring fans.

"You know, if we don't want to watch a horror movie," Sam speaks up, subtly steering the conversation back on track, "we could always watch this new ghost-hunting show that I heard about."

"Ghost-hunting? Pfft," Cory scoffs.

"What, are you saying you don't believe in ghosts, Cornelius?" Josh asks.

"No, I'm saying I don't believe in little boxes that are programmed to beep or contraptions that are rigged to make doors look like they're opening on their own."

"Hear, hear," Oliver agrees.

"Well, I think it sounds interesting," I say.

"I'll watch it as long as it scares my pants off," Josh announces.

"Oh well, in that case, I'll pass, too," I remark.

"Come on, Mel, you love me," Josh retorts.

"Of course I do." You know, like a weird brother. Or a pet.

"Good. Now that you've finally come to terms with your feelings, to the back of the bus!"

Despite their initial skepticism, Joni and the rest of the guys follow Josh, Sam, and me back to the media room. With seven of us, we're sort of packed in like sardines, but we somehow manage to fit all of us on the couches. Much to my delight, I manage to snag a seat next to Sam. I can definitely think of worse ways to spend a night than pressed up against the boy I've been in love with basically my entire life.

Then again, with Josh on my other side, I can't say I'm expecting this to be a romantic evening.

"So what's this show called again?" Josh asks through a mouthful of popcorn.

"*Cemetery Tours*," Sam answers.

"Oh, so it's more of a documentary." Cory sounds a lot more interested now.

"The title is misleading," Sam admits. "The premise is four paranormal investigators travel around to different haunted locations and try to record evidence of ghosts. For example, in this episode, they're trying to make contact with the ghosts of Galveston."

"Huh. Okay. That doesn't sound too bad," Jesse says.

The episode opens with a young man standing on the steps of an old, Victorian-style mansion. He introduces himself as Luke Rainer.

"We're here in Galveston, Texas, arguably one of the most haunted cities in the United States. Known for its blue waters, its sandy beaches, and its historic Pleasure Pier, Galveston is a popular vacation destination for those seeking an island getaway. But the sun hasn't always shone on these idyllic southern shores.

"On September 8th, in the year 1900, a monstrous Category 4 hurricane swept through Galveston, demolishing buildings and wiping out two-thirds of the population. To this day, the Great Storm of 1900 remains the deadliest natural disaster in our nation's history.

"In the three days we've been down here, we've met with local tour guides and island historians. If their stories are to be believed, the entirety of Galveston itself... is a graveyard. Every inch of this island has seen death. That is how devastating the Storm of 1900 was."

"He seems... dramatic," Oliver observes.

"He seems arrogant," Cory grumbles.

"He seems awesome!" Josh grins. "This show is gonna be badass."

"He does seem to have done his research," Joni comments.

"Oh, please," Cory remarks.

"What?" Joni demands.

"This guy hasn't done any research. You just think he's hot."

"Um, excuse me, did I say that?" Joni asks. "Did anyone hear me say that?"

"You didn't have to say anything," Cory argues. "He is *exactly* your type. An over-sexed, over-confident, preppy bad boy."

And now, we are all making a very conscious effort to *not* make eye awkward contact Jesse.

Although I have to admit, this ghost-hunter guy, Luke Rainer, *is* pretty hot. He's older, probably in his late twenties or may even his early thirties, but there's something very charming about his green eyes and blond locks. Maybe it's that he reminds me of Sam. That is if Sam was taller and buffer and dressed like he'd purchased his entire wardrobe from Hot Topic in the early 2000s.

Luke goes on to introduce us to the other three members of the *Cemetery Tours* crew, J.T., Gail, and Peter, before their investigation officially begins. Initially, I hadn't known if I'd be able to take them all that seriously, especially with an overgrown emo kid like Luke leading the way. But halfway through the episode, I realize that Joni had been right all along. They really do know what they're doing. They're not just out there consulting Ouija boards or lighting candles. They measure the electromagnetic field and temperature fluctuations, they analyze every picture and every phantom voice (which they call an EVP), and they even go out of their way to try to disprove their evidence. It's all surprisingly scientific. Even Cory and Oliver are impressed.

Jesse, on the other hand, flinches every time something goes bump in the night... or on the bus.

"Eah! Guys, this is too much," he moans, slouching back against the couch and covering his eyes with his fingers.

"Oh, if only the fans could see their beloved broody bad boy now," Oliver laughs.

"Oliver, has anyone ever told you you've got a real gift for alliteration?" Cory asks.

"It's because he's British," Josh quips.

"Guys, shh!" Joni shushes them.

"Yeah, guys. Joni's new boyfriend is about to do a spirit box session," Sam teases, getting in on the fun.

"Shut up, Sam," Joni snaps.

Tightly packed as we are in here, these are the moments I've missed the most these last couple of months. Before everyone knew the guys' names, before strangers on the sidewalk were singing their songs, this is how we would pass the time. Hanging out. Watching TV shows. Laughing like we didn't have a care in the world. As fun as the celebrity lifestyle and the rock star tour can be, nothing compares to these simple moments of normalcy.

Even if they only last for one night.

Or in this instance, two.

It's Halloween and the guys magically managed to convince their manager, Stan, to give them the night off. It's an All Hallow's Eve miracle. Or perhaps witchcraft.

Either way, I'm not complaining.

Since we're far too old to go Trick-or-Treating, and since the guys can't exactly go door-to-door asking for candy, we've checked into a hotel for an old-fashioned Halloween party. We even managed to grab some cheap costumes from the local Wal-Mart. Sam is a zombie. Cory's a pirate. Oliver is Harry Potter. Jesse is too cool for costumes, apparently. Joni is a witch. And I'm a vampire.

Technically, I'm Alice from *Twilight*, but there's no way I'm admitting that to anyone in this room. They made enough fun of me when they caught me re-reading the books during our senior finals.

And then, finally, there's Josh who is... still changing into his costume. At least, I'm assuming that's where he is. We didn't leave him at Wal-Mart.

While we wait for him to show up, we set out the snacks; fruit and cheese platters, slices of sourdough and French bread, and a sushi platter which I argued was a terrible idea, especially the night before a concert, but whatever. We also have cream soda and sparkling cider since none of us is twenty-one yet. And of course, we have plenty of candy.

Cory has just poured the last glass of sparkling cider when Josh, or at least, the thing I'm assuming is Josh, comes barging in the room. Dressed in a black hooded cloak and hideous demon mask, I think it's safe to say that Josh is really getting in the spirit of the holiday.

"Greetings, mortals!" he booms through his stupid mask. "It is I! Your *doom!*"

"Oh, no... Run for your lives," Jesse snickers.

"Okay, don't even try to act cool, Jesse McScaredy-Pants. We were all there last night," Josh remarks, pointing a skeletal finger at his bandmate.

"So, what's in the bag, oh harbinger of doom?" Sam asks Josh.

It's only then that I notice the plastic Wal-Mart bag partially hidden beneath Josh's billowy black sleeves.

"I'm glad you asked, Mr. Zombie Man," Josh replies. "In this bag, I hold the key to unlocking the secrets of the spirit world, the answer to all of the questions we never dare to ask, the mystic portal to the outer realms... My friends, my fiends, my fellow children of the dark, I present to you... the Ouija board!" he exclaims, displaying the box for all of us to see.

"Oh, that's greatness," Sam laughs.

"Are you serious? What are we, twelve?" Joni asks.

"What? I thought you were into this stuff last night!" Josh says.

"I thought their approach to paranormal investigating was interesting. I never said I wanted to sit around a dumb board and ask it if Bobby Benson was going to take me to Homecoming."

"Ew. You had a thing for Bobby Benson?" Josh wrinkles his nose.

Joni rolls her eyes in response.

"I think it sounds fun. I'm in," Sam announces. "Cory? Ollie?"

"Oh... why not?" Oliver sighs.

"It's Halloween. What the hell," Cory agrees.

"Hey, you guys do what you want. I'm not touching that thing," Jesse says, holding his hands up and taking a step back.

"What? Why not?" Josh asks.

"Because of what you said earlier about the spirit world and portals and all that crap. I don't want to mess with it."

"Come on, Jess, it's not real," Cory laughs.

"You don't know that!" Jesse exclaims.

"Well, we're going to play whether you like it or not," Josh tells him. "Gather 'round, friends! Tonight... we consult the spirit world!"

"If you guys summon a demon, I swear, I will never talk to any of you again," Jesse says, crossing his arms and falling back onto the couch.

"Don't tempt us," Joni mutters under her breath.

Once Josh has the board set up, we all take a seat on the floor around the coffee table.

"So, how does this work?" I ask.

"According to the rules, two of us at a time let our fingers hover over this little pointer thing, and then when we ask it questions it will move to spell out the answer on the board," Josh says.

"By which he means, whoever happens to be playing moves it to the answer they're hoping for," Joni translates.

"You know what, Joni? You just lost your Ouija privileges," Josh says.

"What? You can't do that!"

"It's my board. I can do whatever I want. Now. Who wants to be my co-pilot?" Josh asks, laying his hands over the heart-shaped pointer.

"I will!" To no one's surprise, Sam volunteers.

"Excellent. Come closer, Samuel, and we shall begin."

Sam reaches his hands out, just like Josh. He must feel me watching him because he glances at me out of the corner of his eye and grins.

Oh God, I hope they know what they're doing.

"Okay." Josh takes a deep breath. "Hello, spirits. This is Josh Cahill, international pop sensation and front man for The Kind of September."

"What?" Oliver hisses.

"No, you're not!" Cory objects.

"Guys, they have to think I'm important or they're not going to talk to us," Josh reasons.

"Or they're going to be offended when they find out you're lying to them," Sam argues.

"I'm telling you, you're all going to get cursed," Jesse remarks.

"Don't listen to him, spirits. He's a Slytherin," Josh says. "We are your friends. We open ourselves up to you - "

"Whoa, whoa, hold up. I don't know if I'd go that far," I interrupt.

"Don't worry. I know what I'm doing," Josh insists.

"Do you, though?"

"Have faith, sweet Hufflepuff," Josh tells me.

I don't. Not at all. And for the record, he's a Hufflepuff, too.

"Are you here with us, spirits?" Josh asks.

Beneath their fingers, the pointer slides to Yes.

"Was that you?" Sam asks.

"Nope. You?"

"I'm not even touching it!"

"I'm not, either!" Josh exclaims, a wicked grin on his face. "Okay, okay. Forgive us, spirits. We're excited to speak with you."

"Is it okay if we ask you a few questions?" Sam asks.

Yes.

"All right. Who wants to go first?" Josh asks.

No one speaks up.

"Anyone?" Sam asks.

"Hey, I've got an idea. Why don't we let the fans ask?" Oliver suggests. "We could get a live stream going and have them send in their questions."

"That's actually a great idea," Joni says.

"Oliver, you're a genius!" Josh exclaims. "All right, who wants to live stream for us?"

"I'll do it," Cory volunteers.

"Way to step up to the plate, Cornelius," Josh grins.

"Don't call me that."

"Oh, but it suits you."

Cory shakes his head as he logs into the band's official Instagram account begins the stream.

"Hey what's up, everybody? Happy Halloween! I hope you're all having a wonderful and spooky time - "

"Okay, you're fired," Josh groans, swiping the phone away from Cory. "Witches and werewolves and ghouls of all ages! All Hallow's Eve is upon us! To celebrate this most mystical of nights, we, The Kind of September, have acquired... a Ouija Board! And as a trick or a treat or both, we invite you to cast your questions for us into cyberspace and we will let the spirit world answer." And with that, Josh finally hands Cory back his phone. "*That*'s how you address the crowds on Halloween."

"Guys, questions are already pouring in," Oliver announces, glancing over Cory's shoulder. "So far, the one I'm seeing the most is 'Where's Jesse?'"

"He's over there," Cory answers, holding the phone up so that fans can see Jesse. "He thinks we're going to put a curse on him."

"You are!" Jesse insists.

"Let's see what the spirits have to say about that. Are we going to put a curse on Jesse?" Josh asks the Ouija board.

Yes.

"Ohhh!" All the guys laugh.

"That's not funny. You guys are the worst," Jesse grumbles.

"Okay, okay. Next question," Cory says. "'Will The Kind of September ever tour in the Philippines?'"

"I hope so!" Sam exclaims.

Yes, the board answers.

"Next," Oliver reads. "'Will The Kind of September win a Grammy this year?'"

No.

"Ouch!" Josh laughs. "Harsh, spirits. Harsh!"

"Will we even be nominated?" Sam asks.

No.

"Well, there you have it," Cory quips. "Next question. 'Will Oliver ever fall in love with me?' That's from LucyLollipop98."

"Ohhh!" The guys laugh again.

Yes.

"OHHH!" They whoop even louder.

"Oliver, you DOG!" Josh hollers.

"Lucy, you're a lucky girl," Sam grins.

"Here's another along those lines. 'Does Sam have a secret crush on anyone?'" Oliver reads.

Yes.

"You got me," Sam shrugs.

Even though I know he's probably joking, my heart skips a beat and an irrational sense of dread floods my veins.

"Oh yeah? Who is it?" Cory asks.

"Your mom," Josh responds before he can stop himself.

"Actually, Josiah, it's your mom," Sam remarks.

"Keep dreaming, Morneau. My mom is way out of your league."

The laughter that erupts is so loud that we almost don't hear the distant *Th-thump* from across the room. The room falls silent almost immediately.

"What was that?" I ask.

"Probably nothing," Josh says.

"No. It was something," Jesse tells us, sounding extra uppity. "You guys summoned up a demon and now it's throwing stuff."

"I'm sure it was someone in another room," Oliver says.

"But it sounded like it came from in here," Joni argues.

"Guys, relax," Cory says. "It's probably just - "

Just then, the lights begin to flicker. It's as though the spirits are daring him to finish.

"Oh, *hell* no!" Jesse exclaims. "That's it. I'm done. I'm out of here."

"Where are you going to go? This is *our* room!" Josh reminds him.

"I'll sleep with the girls tonight."

"Like hell you will," Joni snaps.

The lights flicker again. This time, I can't help it. I scream.

But then, something magical happens. Sam grabs my hand. And laces his fingers through mine.

And suddenly, I can't remember how to breathe.

"It's going to be okay," he assures me, scooting over so close to me that our shoulders are touching.

Have I mentioned before that I love Halloween?

"All right, well, I think that's about all the time we have for questions. Love you guys! Happy Halloween!" Cory rambles, ending the live stream.

"Do you think it's still here?" Sam asks.

"I don't know," Josh says. "I guess we could ask the board - "

"No!" Jesse, Cory, and I all holler at once.

"I think... that's enough Ouija for one night." Oliver, ever the voice of reason, tries his best to speak calmly, but I can tell even he's shaken by the strange activity in the room.

"But how are we supposed to sleep in here if there's a demon running loose?" Josh asks.

"Don't ask us! This was all your idea!" Cory reminds him.

The lights flicker once more before the lamp closest to us burns out completely. Again, I shriek. Sam lets go of my hand and wraps both arms around me.

"That's it. I'm sleeping on the bus," Jesse announces.

"You know, I think I might join you," Josh agrees.

"Wait, you're just going to leave us up here?" Cory asks.

"Yep," Josh answers.

"There's safety in numbers, guys," Sam says.

"There are also more bodies for the spirits to draw energy from. Weren't you listening to Luke Rainer last night, Samuel?" Josh asks.

"I never thought I'd agree with Josh, but the bus is sounding better and better," I remark.

"This isn't your room. You don't have to worry," Cory says.

"Yeah, but we're right across the hall," Joni argues.

"If the girls are sleeping on the bus, then I am, too," Sam announces.

"Why?" Cory asks.

"I can't leave them alone with *those* two!" Sam exclaims, indicating Josh and Jesse.

"What's the matter, Samuel?" Josh smirks. "Afraid Mel won't be able to resist climbing into my bunk for a snuggle if you're not there?"

Oh, my God.

"You know what? Forget it," I say. "I'll just stay up here and take my chances with the demon."

Th-thump.

Th-thump.

The words are no sooner out of my mouth than we hear the mysterious noise again, louder, closer, and more distinct. It's only then that I finally recognize the sounds. They're not the sound of a book falling to the ground or a hotel neighbor pounding on the wall.

They're footsteps.

And they're inside the room.

An hour later, all seven of us have showered, changed, and are tucking ourselves into our respective bunks on the tour bus.

"You know, all things considered, this has been kind of a fun Halloween," Sam says, grinning down at me from the bed directly above mine.

"I guess so," I reply. "But next year, I think I'd be okay just eating candy and watching *Hocus Pocus.*"

"And carving jack-o-lanterns," Sam adds.

"That, too."

"Okay, guys, I'm turning off the lights," Joni announces.

"Goodnight, everyone," Jesse yawns from his bunk.

"Goodnight," I reply.

"Happy Halloween," Cory mutters dryly.

Finally, the bus falls silent.

I close my eyes, take a deep breath, and try my best to calm my racing mind. I think about the tour and all the new places we've seen so far this year. I think about the guys' new album they've been writing, *17 Times Over*, and imagine how fans will react to it.

I think about Sam and the way he held me tonight... how warm and safe I felt in his embrace.

Then, just as I finally feel myself beginning to doze off, I hear Josh whisper through the darkness.

"So... anyone want to tell ghost stories?"

A Few Months Later...

Michael Sinclair had no idea what he'd gotten himself into.

Sure, he'd been to concerts in his younger years. He'd seen the Smashing Pumpkins, the Goo Goo Dolls, even the Red Hot Chili Peppers. But none of those experiences had prepared him for the wildly chaotic energy of thousands of teenage fangirls screaming their lungs out for their favorite boy band.

"What are these guys called again?" He had to shout to be heard above the roaring crowd.

"The Kind of September!" Kate hollered back. "Aren't they adorable?"

At twenty-five, Michael's girlfriend, Kate, was a little older than most of the girls in the audience, but she didn't seem to mind at all. In fact, she was having the time of her life cheering, dancing, and even singing along to her favorite songs.

"How old are they?" Michael asked.

"Like, late teens, early twenties," she answered.

"Sweet! We're the same age!" Brink, the eighteen-year-old ghost to Michael's right grinned. "Hey, do you think they'd let me join the band?"

"Can you sing?" Michael asked, knowing all-too-well the answer was no. Years of being the only person capable of listening to Brink's tone-deaf caterwauling had taught him that.

"Oh, like that matters," Brink said with a wave of his hand. "Besides, it's not like you can sing, either."

"That's true, but I'm not thinking of joining a boy band."

"Too bad. It would score you major points with the ladies."

"Wha - ? I don't need to score points with the ladies. I have a girlfriend."

"For now," Brink remarked. "Until she leaves you for Sam Morneau."

"Who's Sam Morneau?" Michael asked.

"Oh, he's the *really* cute one," Kate answered, totally oblivious to the conversation Michael had just had with Brink. "The one with the longish hair and the amazing smile? You know, you kind of look like him."

"What?" Michael laughed. "I've got to be what, ten years older than he is?"

"He could be your little brother, then. I mean, his hair's lighter and you're a lot taller, but you have the same bone structure. And the same big, pretty eyes."

"I don't see it at all, but take it as a compliment and run," Brink advised.

"Well... thank you," Michael said to Kate.

Kate grinned and kissed him swiftly on the cheek before turning her gaze back to the stage.

"Okay, so maybe you're safe for a while," Brink said. "After all, I'm pretty sure you're the only boyfriend here."

He wasn't wrong, Michael noticed. Most of the girls in the audience were there either with their friends or with their dads. He was definitely the odd one out.

"Dallas, thank you so much for your warm welcome!" one of the guys on stage exclaimed into his handheld microphone. "Is everyone having a good time tonight?"

Kate squealed along with the rest of the audience. Michael tried his best not to grimace.

"We are glad to hear it," another guy grinned. This guy, Michael noticed, spoke with a British accent. "All right, this next song is our latest single from our new album. It's called 'Smokescreen.'"

"Oh, hey! I know this song!" Brink exclaimed.

And Michael realized as the guys on stage started singing, that he did, too. He'd heard it on the radio in Kate's car and he'd been surprised by how much he liked it.

"In this world of mirrors
And crystal-clear delusions,
Love is all in what you see
But you hide behind a smokescreen.
These colors drowning out
And these shapes all seem to fade
And I'm struggling to see
Beyond your smile, beyond your smokescreen..."

In the middle of the first refrain, Michael felt Kate take his hand and lace her fingers through his. Then, she rested her head on his shoulder and began to sing softly along with the band.

"Tell me all your secrets and I swear, I'll love you more... I'll protect you from the ghosts you've tried to hide..."

As she sang, Michael glanced down at her, and he couldn't help but smile. The way she lost herself in the music captivated him, and Michael was certain he'd never seen anyone so beautiful.

She must have sensed him watching, because in that moment, she looked up at him. Then, with the glow of a dozen spotlights dancing in her eyes, she rose up on her toes, wrapped her arms around his neck, and kissed him.

Author's Note

Hi, y'all! I hope you've enjoyed this short collection of stories as much as I enjoyed putting it together.

Four of these stories have been featured in anthologies before, but the other four have never been published. While it's my privilege to share them all with you here in one place, I wanted to be sure to tell you about those other titles, just in case you'd like to check them out as well!

The Water's Edge was first published in 2015 by Crushing Hearts and Black Butterfly Publishing in first anthology in the *Lurking* series, *Lurking in the Deep*.

An Empty Building and *Lauren* were also published by CHBB Publishing in the second and third installments of the *Lurking* series, *Lurking in the Shadows* (2016) and *Lurking in the Mind* (2017).

Instinct was published in 2017 in *Ever in the After,* a limited-edition charity anthology, the proceeds of which went to benefit Lift 4 Autism.

Finally, although the story itself has never been published before, *Crossover* features characters from my two series, the *Boy Band* series and the *Cemetery Tours* series. It's a story that I thought would be fun to write for a while now, and I hope it's one that fans of one or both of the series can enjoy.

Oh, and one more thing. While the story *The Kisharliet* has never been published, it's not something that I technically chose to write myself. About a year ago, I was given the very specific prompt to write a science fiction story... in a prison... about a labor union. Now, I would love to tell you that that sort of thing would come naturally to me, but it didn't. Especially the science fiction part.

In the end, I actually ended up rather liking my story, especially considering all the research I put into it to come up with those weird sci-fi names, so I decided to include it here. I hope you enjoyed it. Though, if you didn't, I can't say I blame you. It was a weird prompt.

Acknowledgements

As always, I want to say thank you to my Lord and Savior.

Thank you to my parents, Susie and Dave, for being a constant source of love, support, and encouragement.

Thank you to my sister, KJ, for being my best friend, my traveling companion, and the one who suggested I release this anthology in the first place.

Thank you to my friends, Hannah, Jessica, Aïda, Jalitza, Amanda, and Ashley for your love and for always being there for me. I love you all!

Thank you to my colleagues, my fellow writers, including but not limited to James William Peercy (*The Wall Outside*) and his amanuensis, Claudette, Miracle Austin (*Boundless*), Terri R. Malek (*My Path to Omega*), Cody Wagner (*The Gay Teen's Guide to Defeating a Siren*), April L. Wood (*Winter's Curse*), Kendra L. Saunders (*Dating an Alien Popstar*), Sarah MacTavish (*Firebrand*), Susie Clevenger (*Where Butterflies Pray*) and her husband, Charlie, and so, so, so many others! Thank you for your guiding light and your love!

And finally, thank you to my beautiful, wonderful, amazing readers. There are far too many of you to list, but I'd like to at least mention Honor, Morgan, Natalie, Cassandra, Marine, Danika, Kaylin, Sandra, Lindsey, Marialena, Tamar, Christina, Candice, Camile, Prar, John, … I love you all! You mean the world to me!

© 2017 by Fervent Images – Tim Malek

JACQUELINE E. SMITH is the award-winning author of the CEMETERY TOURS series, the BOY BAND series, and TRASHY ROMANCE NOVEL. A longtime lover of words, stories, and characters, Jacqueline earned her Master's Degree in Humanities from the University of Texas at Dallas in 2012. She lives and writes in Dallas, Texas.

Made in the USA
Columbia, SC
28 February 2020